Assassin

A Sassy Spaceship Captain Adventure

Freelancer 3

Copyright © 2019 by Jane Killick

All rights reserved.

Assassin: Freelancer #3 / Jane Killick

Published by: Elly Books, UK

ISBN: 978-1-908340-31-3

ASSASSIN

FREELANCER 3

JANE KILLICK

Elly Books

Chapter One

ONLY THE CONSPIRATORS knew the assassin lay hidden in the Halls of the Deity. They must have smuggled him and his weapon through security and identified the perfect vantage point for him to unleash the deadly power of his Energy Expenditure Rifle. They must have thought they had planned every last detail and allowed for every eventuality. But they hadn't planned on me. Without me, their conspiracy might never have been revealed.

In truth, I shouldn't have accepted the invitation to the royal wedding in the first place. The man I used to love was getting married to someone else – why would I put myself through that torture? But Freddi persuaded me not to turn down the opportunity to attend the year's most talked about party on Fertilla. It was a chance, he said, to mingle with the great and good of several planetary systems and to take advantage of the free food and booze – all at the royal family's expense.

Freddi and I stepped out of the hideously expensive transport vehicle we had hired to bring us from Londos spaceport to the centre of the city and stood in front of the Halls of the Deity.

With its magnificent towers which reached up to the enclosed roof of the city, it was the most striking building on the whole of Fertilla. It was constructed using five circular turrets which interlocked with each other as they rose up to brush the underneath of the artificial sky with their golden-domed roofs. The building had been erected by an early settler with as much religious fervour as he had money, who donated it to the Monks of the Deity as a base for their charitable works. Since then, although the black-robed order still nominally ran the place, it was used primarily as a functional building for important and state occasions.

Such was the marriage of Prince Stephen Regellan of Fertilla to Helinea, sister to the ruling president of Manupia.

Freddi looked so different in the clothes he had chosen for the occasion. I was used to seeing him in practical scuffed trousers and shabby jacket as we worked freelance jobs on my spaceship. The neat version, in a pristine deep blue suit with pure white shirt, was quite a contrast. He had shaved all trace of stubble from his face and had actually paid someone in Londos to cut the strands of his ginger and grey hair so they hung to just below his ears.

"Wedding attire really suits you," I told him.

"No it doesn't, Cassy," he said. "I only made the effort so they'd let me in with you."

I was wearing the stunning blue dress I had worn on the last day I had seen Stephen. He had given it to me for a party at Londos House which I had fled after clashing with his mother. I only kept the dress because I didn't know what else to do with it. When I put it on again, I remembered the first time I saw myself wearing it in the mirror of Stephen's bedchamber. I had felt sexy and loved in the shimmering blue material which followed the curves of my body from the low neckline, across my breasts, in at the waist and out into a full, ankle-length skirt. Like the first time, I had twisted my hair into a tidy braid which rested across my collarbone. Nearly a year later, the same image of myself made me feel uncomfortable. I would have preferred to let my dark hair flow freely down to the bottom of my shoulder blades while wearing my regular spacefaring trousers and shirt with my Energy Expenditure Weapon strapped to my thigh. But such an outfit would have had me barred from the event – if not arrested.

The pedestrian entrance was packed with people all equally dressed up for the occasion. We passed through two checkpoints staffed by Fertillan Guard who looked carefully at our invitations and identification. The third checkpoint included a weapons detector and Freddi had his fifteen-centimetre-long knife – which he had concealed in his inside pocket – confiscated by a tall Fertillan Guardswoman who looked quite beautiful despite her unflattering brown uniform. She gave him the most filthy look from the beneath the peak of her cap, but waved us through before turning to deal with the next person in the queue.

"What did you bring a knife for?" I asked Freddi as we walked away from the weapons detector.

"Habit," he said.

I laughed. Several of the other guests looked down their noses at me as if it were inappropriate to be happy at such a momentous event, but I didn't care. It made me feel better that I wasn't part of their snobby elite.

3

It was breathtaking to look up inside the main tower. The underside of the domed roof was encrusted with cut glass lit by a central globe light which sent tiny rainbows radiating out onto the surrounding curved walls. Further down were mini-balconies coming off the wall like little viewing platforms where a handful of people could watch proceedings from their own vantage points. Between them hung drapes of rich red material which disguised the plainness of the walls and deadened the noise which would otherwise have echoed back off the hard surface. At various places around the hall were technicians with cameras ready to capture the spectacle of the royal wedding for all the galaxy to witness.

Rows of seats in regimented formation were laid between us and a grand stage at the front adorned with waist-high vases of fresh, green foliage dotted with the tiny white heads of flowers. Between us and the seating area was yet another team of Fertillan Guards who were showing the guests to their allotted places.

I retrieved my P-tab from where I had put it away in the folds of my dress and showed it to a guard whose jacket buttons were having a hard time containing his ample belly.

He looked up from my name on the invitation and stared at my face. "Individual Sesaan Cassandra?"

Even though I was entitled to be there, the way he said it caused a flurry of nerves. "Yes."

With that confirmation, he waved to another one of the guards to take over from him.

Freddi and I exchanged wary glances.

"Come with me," said the plump guard.

"Where?" I demanded.

"This way." He put his hand in the small of my back – firmly, but not aggressively – and guided me towards the side of the hall.

Freddi followed, but the guard put out a hand to stop him. "Just Individual Cassandra."

"It's okay, Freddi," I said.

"Are you sure?"

"Yes," I said, but it was a lie. I was nervous that my not entirely blameless life had left something undesirable on my record which made me unsuitable as a royal wedding guest. Although, as far as I could remember, I hadn't done anything illegal on Fertilla – yet.

The guard pushed me forward again and, despite my reservations, I allowed myself to be propelled away from Freddi. When I looked back, I caught only a brief glimpse of his concerned expression before other wedding guests moved in between us and he disappeared from view.

"What is this about?" I asked the guard.

"I've been told to bring you," was all he said.

I was taken through a side door – flanked by two armed Fertillan Guards on sentry duty – into a part of the building which was utilitarian in contrast to the grandeur of the main hall. We were in a length of plain corridor with a low ceiling, lit by dimly glowing lights which illuminated the path to more, plain, unmarked doors.

They made me even more nervous and I stopped. "Where are we going?"

"This way," said the guard, stepping forward.

"No." I stood my ground.

The guard grabbed at my wrist. "You need to come this way."

"Not until you tell me what the vac is going on!" I pulled my wrist back from his grasp.

"My orders are–"

"I don't care about your orders. *I* haven't been ordered to do anything! I have an official invitation. Look–" I held my P-tab out towards him, but before he had the chance to look, one of the doors opened.

A man's face peered out into the corridor. "What the vac is going on?"

I recognised him immediately. It was Prince Stephen. I sighed with relief at seeing him, but my nerves didn't settle.

"Sire." The guard snapped to attention. "I have brought Individual Sesaan Cassandra, Sire."

Stephen took half a step out into the corridor and I had my first glimpse of the gold-embroidered black suit he was wearing for his wedding day. "Cassy!" he called out and gave me a friendly wave. "You came. I'm so pleased."

I turned and gave the guard a foul look as the man was dismissed. Stephen then invited me into the room which lay behind the plain door.

"By the Deity, Stephen," I said as I stepped inside. "I thought I was being arrested!"

"Sorry if my staff were being over-zealous. I asked them to look out for you when you arrived."

I forced myself to relax so I could take in the small room where we were standing. Like the corridor, it was relatively plain, but some effort had been made to turn it into a comfortable space. There was a sofa, a table with the remains of Stephen's lunch on it and a full-length mirror where I caught a glimpse of myself in my long, blue dress.

Stephen looked as regal as ever. The gold embroidery down the lapels of his suit glittered in the bright light of the room and might have looked ostentatious on another man, but he wore it with the confidence of a prince. Underneath, a tailored light brown shirt was buttoned up to his neck where it finished in the clean line of a stiff collar. His brown hair had been recently cut into its usual military style, his chin was smooth and freshly shaved and even the wide nose that his family was known for seemed in proportion to his face. But it was his blue eyes, and how they looked at me in the same way they had done when we were lovers, which were the most striking.

"I see you're wearing the dress I gave you," he said.

"I couldn't afford a new one."

I tried to maintain my stoic exterior as my insides remembered how we had once laughed together and enjoyed the bliss of sharing our bodies.

"I wasn't sure you would come to the wedding."

"I wasn't sure either," I said. "But Freddi said we couldn't turn down the chance of a free party."

He smiled. "How is Freddi?"

"Probably panicking that I was taken away by one of your Fertillan Guards."

"Then I won't keep you long. I asked to see you because we never had the chance to talk after your encounter with my mother."

"Maybe I didn't want to talk to you about it." The memory of what she said at the royal party still hurt. It was when I found out that she had ordered my own mother be burnt to death and the murder covered up so it looked like a tragic house fire. Up until that moment – for all of my childhood and into my adult life – I had thought my mother had died in an accident.

"I didn't know what my mother had done, Cassy, I swear. I was only a boy when it happened."

7

"It doesn't matter whether you knew or not, Stephen. It's not something I can forgive."

He looked crestfallen, and fiddled nervously with the gold embroidery on the lapel of his jacket. "I still would like to apologise on behalf of my family. I know you are not ready to accept my apology – perhaps you never will be – but I wanted to offer it in any case. I don't imagine we'll get the chance to see each other after I'm married."

"No," I said. "Is she nice, this woman you're marrying?"

"Helinea?" said Stephen. "She seems to be, on the couple of occasions I've met her."

"You've only met your wife-to-be twice?"

"I'm sure it's no secret that it's an arranged marriage. It will help secure a political alliance between our two planets. The ceremony is a chance for a public celebration and for the whole galaxy to see that the interests of Fertilla and Manupia are linked."

He spoke with impassive honesty that held no joy.

"You don't sound like you're looking forward to it," I said.

"My feelings are irrelevant. It is my duty."

"And her feelings?"

"She understands the need for the marriage. She said she hopes, in time, we might develop an affection for each other. She expressed the desire to have children and I think that having a family will be good for me."

I had hoped that attending the wedding of my ex-lover would draw a line under our relationship. That there would be a beautiful ceremony, I would get drunk, gorge myself on free food and finally turn my back on that part of my life. But, instead, seeing him again was reawakening feelings I had hidden away and tried to forget.

"I need to go, Stephen."

"Cassy, wait…"

I stopped halfway to the door and he came up close behind me so I could feel his presence at my back.

"I wish things could be different," he said.

"Me too," I heard myself say. I turned back round to face him and he was close enough for me to smell his masculinity and how it intertwined with the perfume of his aftershave.

"But I am a prince and I have my duty," he said.

"And I am a freelance spaceship captain and I have a life a long way away from the royal household."

"It never would have worked between us two, would it?" he said. "Even if my mother had never spoken to you."

I shook my head. "No. I don't think so."

"Then you should go back to the main hall," said Stephen, stepping back and giving me space to open the door. "And, when they hand round the drinks, I would like to think that you will raise a toast to me and Helinea and wish us well."

"Of course I will, Stephen."

I turned back to the door and grasped the handle. I tried to think of something else to say, but there were no words, only unfulfilled emotions, and so I let myself out of his room and stepped back into the corridor.

IN THE BLANDNESS of the corridor, the heat of my emotions rushed to my skin and I had to lean back against the cold wall. The little box where I had locked up my love for Stephen had been forced open and spilled its contents into my bloodstream. I hadn't wanted to admit it, but I still loved him.

I took a minute to compose myself. I breathed deep and rebuilt the walls of my stoic exterior.

As calm returned, the memory of Freddi's concerned face in the crowded hall came back to me. I pulled out my P-tab and sent him a message to say I was fine and hadn't been arrested.

I was about to go back into the main hall to find him, but after a few steps I realised I had no appetite for watching Stephen get married to another woman and so I sent Freddi another message to say I was going to have a wander round and I would find him later.

I went back the way I had come, past the door to Stephen's room, past another plain door where Helinea might be preparing for her wedding day, and to the end where a set of spiral stairs led up to another level. The sound of footsteps rushing down towards me made me fear I would be discovered by a guard who would escort me back into the hall whether I liked it or not. But the footsteps didn't belong to a guard; they belonged to a monk. His long black robes flowed out behind him as he ran and the hood covering his head was pushed back to reveal his face. He glanced at me, but said nothing as he hurried past.

I climbed the stairs, hitching up my skirt to stop myself tripping over it, until I reached another bland corridor. It was almost a mirror image of the one below, except the doors were on the inside of the curve which bent round to reflect the shape of the main hall. Up ahead, what appeared to be a family group were being led through one of the doors by a woman in Fertillan Guard uniform. A portly grey-bearded gentleman, a bejewelled woman in a long, flowing dress and three children in their finery all disappeared inside while the guard waited by the door before closing it behind them. I thought she would look up the corridor, see me and escort me to the cheap seats where I belonged. But she was concentrating on the task in hand and didn't seem to notice me at all as she turned back the way she had come.

The doors had to lead to the viewing balconies which I had seen from the main hall. I walked past them, counting each door as I went and wondering who were the privileged few sitting behind them. At the fifth door, I stopped. It had been left slightly ajar. I peeked inside to see its plush – and empty – interior.

I went in.

It was a small, carpeted room which looked down onto the full grandeur of the main hall. The crush of invitees below had been sorted out into orderly rows which sat facing the stage. On the stage itself, clustered to one side, was a quartet of string musicians. They bowed their instruments with sustained tuning notes which sang out over the hubbub of chattering voices and shuffling guests.

The balcony was a good vantage point to watch the ceremony. As no one else had claimed it, I decided it would be a waste for it not to be occupied and sat on one of the four red velvet-covered chairs. I leant back and imagined I was rich and important. It also allowed me some privacy in that, should my stoic exterior slip while Stephen took his wedding vows, no one would be there to see it.

The random tuning notes of the string quartet fizzled out, the chatting and the shuffling got louder in expectation, then all four instruments played in harmony. The sweet sound of singing strings drifted up to my box in a beautiful melody I hadn't heard before. I leant forward and laid my forearms across the raised edge of the balcony and watched as the musicians' bows danced in unison to create their heavenly music and enthral the audience into silence.

From the back of the stage came a line of people led by King Richard, who was instantly recognisable from his bearded face. Close behind him was Queen Triana, the woman he had married the previous year who was now looking very pregnant. Prince James followed, wearing a dark grey suit with gold embroidery at the shoulder which was enough to convey his royal status without overshadowing the groom. Then came Sophea, the President of Manupia, who was with a man I didn't know. Bringing up the rear was the very frail figure of the Queen Mother who was almost carried by two royal aids who held onto each of her arms as they helped her to a chair on the opposite side of the stage to the quartet.

The others remained standing and looked in expectation down the length of the hall towards the main entrance.

After only a moment, from behind the rows of seated guests, came a man dressed in white robes who walked up the aisle towards the stage. He was like a photo negative of the black-clad monks who ran the Halls of the Deity. His clothes were of exactly the same style, but made in a more delicate, flowing fabric that swung gracefully with each step. Like the monks, his robe included a hood, but he wore it down so it sat unobtrusively on his shoulders and, from where I was sitting, allowed me to see the bald patch developing around the crown of his blonde hair. He was the Supreme Monk. One of the few people considered to have enough authority to officiate at the marriage of a member of the royal family.

When he reached the stage, an enchanted gasp rose from the crowd as they all turned to look behind them. I inched forward on my seat and craned my neck to see what they were looking at. Prince

Stephen soon came into view, walking up the aisle hand-in-hand with Helinea. She wore the most amazing dress which sparkled with jewels sewn in swirling patterns across the ivory white of the fabric. The tight bodice plunged deep at her neckline and flowed out in a full skirt which swished as she walked. Two puffed sleeves sat on her shoulders and she was crowned with a small, understated tiara which nestled into the long curls of her light brown hair. I understood why the congregation was enchanted: she looked beautiful.

On reaching the stage, the Supreme Monk turned and bowed to them both before telling the assembled people about the glory of marriage.

I sat back and listened to the lies. Maybe marriage was glorious if two people truly loved each other. But in a marriage of convenience, his words sounded hollow.

The door to the balcony clicked open.

I sat up and turned, expecting to see a member of the Fertillan Guard who was going to chuck me out, or a late and flustered dignitary who would claim the box for himself.

Instead, it was a hooded monk in black robes. He looked even more startled to see me than I was to see him.

He glared and waved me out. I reluctantly stood from the soft, plush seat which had been so comfortable and went over to the door while he waited, impatiently, with his hands on his hips. I stepped into the corridor and turned back to get my last look at the ceremony from above. Not that I could see much because the monk was blocking my view.

He moved to shut the door behind me and the movement caused the outer flap of his robe to part and reveal the flash of something metal underneath. I only saw it for a split second, but the gleam of the barrel of an EE Rifle is unmistakable.

I thrust out my foot and jammed it in the doorway before the monk could shut me out.

He bashed the door against my foot, but I pushed back hard. Caught by surprise, he stumbled backwards and I forced my way in.

The sound of singing filled the hall as the wedding guests – oblivious to the gunman above – broke into the familiar, rousing Fertillan anthem to the exuberant accompaniment of the string quartet.

I reached for where I thought the monk's rifle was hidden beneath his robes, but he was there before me, pulled out the weapon and swung it round so the barrel hit me in the face.

I fell backwards and my head smacked hard against the wall of the booth. My vision blurred. I must have cried out, but my voice was lost amid the enthusiastic singing that filled the hall.

Blinking away the threat of concussion, I focussed to see the monk kneeling ready to fire with the barrel of his rifle resting on the edge of the balcony and aimed at the stage.

"No!" I screamed and lunged for him.

A blast shot out of his rifle as I barged into his body and knocked him sideways.

Screams pierced through the singing beneath us, as some people realised what was going on and others kept belting out the anthem.

I reached for the monk's rifle, but he pulled it away and my hand only succeeded in swiping at his face. The nail of my middle finger gouged through the skin with a sickening rip that left a blood-red line carved into his cheek. He screamed, but his voice was just one of many in the hall of increasingly panicked people.

The distraction was enough for me to reach for the gun again, and this time I grabbed hold of the barrel. We tussled for control of the weapon – he elbowed me in the eye – but I kept hold as he squeezed the trigger. A hot pulse of energy surged through the barrel beneath my fingers and fired up into the dome. The blast seared through the encrusted glass ceiling, destroying the tiny rainbows and sending a cascade of splinters onto the crowd below.

He yanked the rifle from my grasp and brought the barrel down towards my face.

"Free Manupia!" he cried. I turned to escape the blow, but not quickly enough, and the butt of his gun struck me hard on the back of my head.

I crashed to the floor with the sounds of screaming and shouting distorting around me. Flashes of light blinked before my vision as I tried to push myself up. But my arms didn't have the strength to hold my body weight and I collapsed.

I must have lost consciousness because the next thing I was aware of I was lying on the floor of the box, staring up at a blurry ceiling with something heavy on my lap. I put my hand on it and felt the cold, hard metal of an EE rifle. I pushed it off me and it landed with a thud on the carpeted floor. Fighting dizziness and a rising nausea, I pulled myself to sitting. No one else was in the booth with me, but from the sound of pandemonium in the hall, I hadn't been out of it for many minutes. Struggling to my knees, I tried to stand up, but stood on the hem of my dress and fell forward. I caught the edge of the balcony to stop myself crashing back to the floor. Peering over the edge, I saw the throngs of wedding guests pushing in panic to flee out of the exits. All except a few who were clustered around the stage. In the centre of them lay the body of Queen Triana: sprawled and unmoving in a pool of blood.

The door to the box burst open and a squadron of Fertillan Guards charged in with their EEWs drawn. I gasped and looked down at the rifle which the assassin had left. The chill of fear surged through my body. Even if I could reach it and aim it, the guards would kill me before I could fire.

"Hands up!" ordered the lead guard, whose weapon was aimed directly at my chest.

I had no option but to obey. The only method of escape, apart from the door which they blocked, was to jump over the balcony and fall to certain death or serious injury.

"I didn't do it," I said, feeling my hands tremble as I held them up at my shoulders.

"I'm arresting you on suspicion of the attempted murder of Queen Triana of Fertilla," said the lead guard.

"It wasn't me!"

He holstered his weapon, while the others kept their EEWs aimed at my chest, and stepped towards me. He grabbed my wrist and encased it with the jaws of a handcuff.

"I didn't try to kill her," I protested. "I didn't try to kill anyone. It was the monk. He did it. You need to go after him!"

But my protests were ignored. The guard roughly spun me round where he handcuffed my other wrist so my hands were secured behind my back. He grabbed my upper arm and, with bruising force, pulled me out of the box to take me to a Fertillan Guard cell.

Chapter Two

THE ACRID SMELL of stale sweat from former prisoners hung in the cell. The jail complex had been dug out of the rock of the Fertillan surface and lined with an impermeable layer of grey evi-plastic to keep the breathable air inside. I had nothing but a bed barely wider than a bench and padded with the thinnest of mattresses, a blanket to keep me warm and a bucket to use if I needed to relieve myself. The only break in the evi-plastic-coated walls was a heavy metal door with a spyhole at eye level.

I sat on the bed and contemplated my fate. For many hours.

I was in a daze of my own melancholy when the sound of the metal shutter sliding back from the spyhole brought me to my senses. Two brown eyes looked at me for a moment before the spyhole was closed again and the door was unlocked.

I stood and felt the material of my dress ruffle down to my ankles.

The brown-eyed Fertillan Guard came into my cell. Behind him was another man who was instantly recognisable as a member of the Regellan royal family with his brown hair, blue eyes and wide nose. It was Prince James, brother to Stephen.

He looked stressed and tired with a five o'clock shadow of stubble emerging on his chin. He still had on the same, dark grey suit as he had worn at the wedding which had crumpled in the many hours since the shooting. Whatever had happened in the intervening time, he obviously hadn't had the chance to wash or change and there was still a streak of dried blood visible on his right sleeve.

"When I heard it was you, I had to come and see for myself," said James.

"It wasn't me," I insisted. "I didn't do anything."

"Why deny it? You were caught with the murder weapon. It has your fingerprints and DNA all over it."

I had let samples be taken from me after my arrest, assuming they would help prove my innocence, and not be used to fabricate my guilt. "Murder?"

"Queen Triana died," said James. "Doctors tried to save her baby, but it was too late."

I put my hand out to the wall to steady myself. "I didn't shoot her, you have to believe me. Why would I want to shoot her?"

"You were obviously trying to kill Helinea of Manupia and missed."

"That's ridiculous!"

"Is it?" James turned to the guard who had come in with him. "You can leave us now."

The guard hesitated, but James's stare was unwavering.

"Sire," he said, bowed and backed out.

"It makes sense that my brother's whore would try to kill his future wife," said James.

I didn't let his usual insult unnerve me. "Your information is out of date. Until the day of the wedding, Stephen and I hadn't seen each other for almost a year."

"Enough time for your jealousy to fester into the desire for murder."

"I had no desire to kill anyone. It was the monk. He had the rifle hidden under his robes. I tried to stop him and we fought over the weapon, that's why my fingerprints and DNA are on it."

"That's a poor alibi, even for a whore."

"It's true," I said. "If I was making up a story, I would have thought of a better one."

"You understand you will be facing the death penalty for this heinous crime," said James.

A rush of fear came over me. "But I'm innocent!"

"You're guilty, Cassy, and the Fertillan courts will prove it. Take this as notice that you will meet your death very soon. In a case like this, justice will be very swift."

He exited and the metal door clanged shut behind him. My legs were no longer able to hold my weight and I flopped down to sit on the bed. The true horror of my situation had only begun to sink in as the locks of the cell door clicked into place and I was left alone in my incarceration.

THE DOOR OF the Fertillan Guard transport was thrown open and I faced a crowd of angry faces who stood between me and the courthouse.

"*Murderer!*" shouted one.

"*Traitor!*" shouted another.

With my hands cuffed in front of me, a guard held onto my upper arm with a grip so tight it squeezed down to the bone, and pulled me forward. When I stepped down, I almost tripped on the stupid dress I was still wearing and it was only the guard's hold that kept me upright.

The crowd pushed in. Like they were trying to get a better look at me, or lynch me, or both. All of them shouting insults in a mass of unintelligible rage. Someone spat at me and their cold, slimy saliva landed on my cheek.

I wiped it off onto my sleeve and tried to maintain my outer dignity while I sensed the mob were moments away from tearing me to pieces. I held up my cuffed wrists to protect my face, but I knew it was futile. I fe

lt helpless and terrified.

A surge from the crowd jostled me sideways. My face collided with the solid chest of the guard at my side and my chin brushed against the roughness of the brown material of his uniform. He pushed me back again and I staggered forward as I was buffeted by the angry horde.

From somewhere at the back of the crowd, the shouts coalesced into chanting.

"*Kill the murderer! Hang the traitor!*"

Their bloodthirsty intent was gaining momentum.

The guard yanked me forward and I thought he was going to

deliver me to the mob, but then I saw a line of brown uniforms reaching out before me.

New, authoritative voices shouted above the chants of the populace: "Make way! By order of the King! Make way!"

At least ten Fertillan Guardsmen had somehow cleared a path to the courthouse. Linking arms, they formed a narrow passage through the crowd to an open, waiting door. I allowed myself to be led through the passageway, feeling its fragility as the crowd pushed in from either side and the path narrowed and shifted from left to right.

Eventually, I was pushed into the courthouse. The toughened glass door closed behind me and the sound of the murderous masses dulled into an ugly, clamouring noise. The Fertillan Guardsmen who had formed my precarious path remained on the other side of the door to protect the building. They formed another chain of linked arms which created a wall of brown with their uniform jackets pressed up against the glass.

That's when I saw Freddi's worried face. Somehow, he had pushed himself to the front of the crowd and, being shorter than most people, was able to stare in at me from under the armpits of the guards' outstretched arms.

Get me out of this, I mouthed to him.

I don't know if he saw or if he understood because I was pulled away and dragged further inside.

I passed through a security checkpoint, was funnelled down a thin corridor and up a flight of steps to a door with a sign that read, 'Prisoner Entrance'.

Shivering at the thought of my new designation, I was led through to a boxed-in platform in the court.

It was about the same size as the box in the Halls of the Deity, except it was plain and solid rather than plush and comforting. A wall up to waist height enclosed me on three sides with thick glass above it so I could see out and others could see in, but I couldn't jump over the barrier and escape.

I caught a reflection of myself in the glass and saw the mess of my hair and a large, brown/purple bruise around my left eye where the monk had elbowed me in the face.

Murmurs from those assembled greeted my arrival as everyone turned to look. Lawyers and court officials in their sombre, black suits sat at a row of desks in the front. Behind them, journalists focussed their cameras and recording equipment on me while other people who had come to watch were crammed onto benches at the back. In the centre of those benches sat Prince James, flanked by two Fertillan Guards. He had neatened himself up and changed into a clean suit since his visit to my cell.

"All rise!" said one of the court officials and the assembled people shuffled to their feet. Even Prince James.

A woman, in a suit as black and sombre as the lawyers', but with a trim of red around the lapels to denote her authority, emerged from a side door and strode onto the raised platform at the front of the courtroom. She took her seat behind a desk from where she could oversee everyone.

The assembled people took her lead and sat down again. I had no chair and remained standing.

When she looked at me, her face was devoid of emotion. "You are Individual Sesaan Cassandra?"

I opened my mouth, but it was too dry to allow me to speak.

The guard nudged me in the ribs. I swallowed and found some

saliva from somewhere. "Yes," I said.

"Speak up!" she demanded. "And you will address me as, 'Your Honour'."

I found enough breath in my lungs to project my words. "Yes, Your Honour."

"You are charged with the murder of Queen Triana and child destruction in relation to the death of her unborn baby, a boy who their Royal Highnesses were planning to name Jonni. Do you understand the charges?"

"I didn't do it," I said.

"That's not what I asked you, Individual Cassandra! You will get the opportunity to enter a plea at a later date. Do you understand the charges?"

"Yes, but I didn't kill anyone!"

"I am remanding you into custody. You will return to court in a week's time."

"What? No!" I pushed forward so I was as close to the judge as possible without squashing my face up against the glass. "I tried to stop him!"

"The prisoner will be silent!" ordered the judge.

She stood and the rest of the court rose to its feet.

I turned to them. I pleaded with them. "It was a man. He said, 'free Manupia'. I tried to stop him! I tried to stop him!"

The guard pulled me back from the glass. I struggled to break free, but he held me tight.

"You have to believe me!"

"*Liar!*" cried a voice from the benches.

"*Murderer!*"

"*Traitor!*"

My determination to stay and scream my innocence was no match for the brute strength of the guard. He pulled me out into the corridor and, as I was led away, the only voices I heard were from the people who had already decided I was guilty.

WHEN I RETURNED to my cell, I found a pile of clothes neatly folded up on the bed.

My clothes.

The ones I had changed out of before the royal party where I had first worn the long blue dress almost a year before. On the same day that I had ran out on Stephen. I had left them behind in his bedchamber and thought I would never see them again.

Yet, there they were. Freshly laundered and waiting for me.

With my back to the spyhole, I threw off the dress and stepped into the wonderfully clean and fresh shirt, trousers and jacket which instantly felt part of me. Although my body was grimy from stress and from not being able to wash, the cleanliness of the clothes and their smooth fabric against my skin made me feel stronger.

I kicked the dress, and all it represented, into the corner of the cell and sat on the bed. Delving my hands deep into the pockets of the jacket to warm my fingers, I touched something pushed into the corner. It was thin and flat and, as I pulled it out, I saw it was a small folded piece of paper.

I unravelled it to see someone had written something on it in block capitals. There were just two words:

"*BE READY.*

CHAPTER THREE

EYES GLARED AT me through the spyhole. The bolts securing my cell door were unlocked.

I stood up to face whatever guard was coming in to fetch me. But it was not a guard. It was Prince Stephen.

I opened my mouth to speak, but he flashed me a look that insisted I kept quiet. My mouth closed as he pushed the door shut behind him and listened for the guard outside to retreat.

Stephen was in sombre, casual clothes which were almost entirely covered up by a dirt-brown cloak that hung from his shoulders down to his mid-calf.

"Tell me you didn't do it, Cassy." He kept his voice low so it was almost a whisper.

"I didn't do it," I said, hoping there was enough sincerity in those four words to convince him.

He nodded, he looked away from me like he was thinking, then fixed me with an intense stare. "I heard what you said in court,

Cassy, but I want you to tell me personally what happened. Tell me everything."

So I told him about the balcony and the monk. I told him about the rifle, how I tried to stop the monk from firing it and how he knocked me unconscious by hitting me across the back of my head.

Stephen lifted his hand up to my black eye and touched the bruised skin. His touch was gentle, even sensual, but my eye was tender and I winced as I pulled back from him. "I was told you got that when you resisted arrest."

"There were five armed Fertillan Guards and I was still concussed from being knocked out. I didn't resist."

"There will be a trial," said Stephen. "Your DNA and fingerprints on the murder weapon will be enough to convict you."

"But I am innocent!"

"It doesn't matter," said Stephen. "The whole planet has already decided you are guilty. The trial is the focus for the public's anger, it is not an arbiter of truth. They say you were motivated by jealousy because I was marrying Helinea and you didn't care who in the royal family you killed, as long as it stopped the ceremony. James will make sure our affair is laid out in the courtroom for all of Fertilla to hear because he thinks it will embarrass me. There will be calls for Fertilla to drop its moratorium on the death penalty. King Richard is so distraught at the death of his wife and unborn son, he will sanction it."

The frisson of hope I had felt when Stephen came into my cell faded away and was replaced with a fear that turned me cold. "I didn't do it, Stephen. You have to believe me."

"I believe you," he said.

"Then you have to get me out of here!"

"I know."

I sighed with relief.

"But you have to understand, you will be a fugitive," he said. "You will have to leave Fertilla and never return. If you go on the run, it will seem to everyone as an admission of guilt."

"Better than the torture of a show trial and being put to death."

Stephen nodded. "I can get you out, but it has to be tonight."

"How?" I said.

"This is a Fertillan Guard facility and I am the head of the Fertillan Guard. That bit is easy enough. After that, I can get you to the spaceport, but you can't leave in your shuttle because you'll be stopped before you even lift off. I would offer you one of my ships, but I'm not sure I can trust even one of my most loyal crews. So I will need to give you money to a buy a no-questions-asked passage on an independent ship."

"Not a problem," I said. I knew several dubious off-worlders who would take a fugitive from Fertilla for the right price.

"It means I won't see you again, Cassy."

"I want to live, Stephen. I can't face a public execution."

He took my hand. "Then come with me."

Pushing open the cell door, he led me out into the corridor. It was empty. In all my comings and goings, there had always been guards stationed there. Stephen must have used his authority to dismiss them.

He closed and locked the cell door behind us, so everything looked normal, and we went past all the other locked cell doors in the corridor to where a metal gate which led to the jail was usually locked. It opened easily with just the push of Stephen's hand and we climbed the stairs into the main complex.

"Stay close behind me." He let go of my hand and I fell in behind the billowing fabric of his cloak as he escorted me down the route I recognised led to the transports at the back of the facility. It was a short maze of passageways that gave a prisoner no chance to break free and was – like the cell corridor – eerily devoid of Fertillan Guards.

Emerging at the back of the building, into the semi-dark of the evening, I saw the same row of transports as I had seen the day I was bundled into the back of one of them and taken to court. All apart from one at the end, which was an official car painted in Fertillan Guard brown which the princes used to travel around Londos. Stephen nodded towards it. Normally, it would have a chauffeur, but I saw through the windscreen that the driver's seat was empty, which meant Stephen was going to drive.

The grit of the city crunched beneath our feet and we headed towards the car. But he stopped short as a figure stepped out from behind it. His face was in shadow, but I knew from the cut of his expensive grey suit and the way he wore it with a sense of superiority that it was Prince James.

"Stevie," he said with disapproval.

I glanced across at the spaces between the other vehicles and considered ways that we could make it out on foot.

"Get out of my way, James," said Stephen.

James merely put his hands into his trouser pockets and relaxed into his stance to suggest he wasn't going anywhere.

"What are you doing with our sister-in-law's murderer, Stevie?"

"Don't interfere," Stephen warned him.

"It seems to me, you are the one who is interfering," said James.

I pressed myself close into Stephen's back and whispered in his ear: "We need to run."

I pulled at his hand, but before we had moved, Fertillan Guards stepped out from between each of the other vehicles and, one by one, unholstered their sidearms.

Four EEWs were aimed in our direction and suddenly all of our escape routes were cut off.

"She's not a murderer," said Stephen.

"Isn't that for the court to decide?" said James.

"A court presided over by a judge who uses the name of King Richard's unborn son to raise emotions against a woman who is innocent until proven guilty? How can I trust an institution like that to be impartial?"

"Stop thinking with your dick, Stevie. Think of the honour of our family."

While the brothers squared up to each other, I concentrated on the armed guards. There were four of them and two of us. I had no weapon and I sensed Stephen wasn't armed either. We could have had a chance if we'd made a break for it, overpowered one of the guards and used the vehicles as cover. But the chances of getting into Stephen's car and driving away without being killed were slim. If we'd tried to run without the speed and power of a vehicle, our chances would have been even slimmer.

"You are a fool if you think these Fertillan Guards will shoot me," said Stephen. "I am their commanding officer."

"Who is harbouring a traitor to the King," added James.

Stephen held out the material of his cloak and wrapped me up in it. He pulled me close and pressed me against the firmness of his torso. I clung tight to my royal human shield and hoped it was enough to protect me.

"You all know me!" Stephen called out to the guards. "I am Marshal Commander Regellan. I order you to stand down."

The guards didn't move. Their guns remained trained on us. Yet, I sensed their unease.

"Arrest them!" yelled James.

The guard on the far right took half a step towards us, but the others stood their ground and he faltered.

"You see," said Stephen to his brother. "They know where their loyalties lie."

"They should be loyal to the King!"

This rattled the guards. Two of them strengthened their grip on their weapons as if they were ready to shoot and the other two followed their example. I knew we had limited time to stand and argue before they turned against us. With my arm around Stephen's waist, I urged him forward, but he wasn't ready to move yet.

"I'm going to walk out of here," Stephen declared to the guards. "And you're going to let me go."

"You are to arrest the traitor by any means necessary!" James countered.

"Think about it!" said Stephen, looking around at each guard and staring directly into their eyes. "Injure a royal prince and you will be the one who is arrested and put on trial for treason. Don't think you can rely on James to protect you because he only cares about you as long as he can use you."

Stephen stepped forward and took me with him. He headed straight for the guard on the left who kept his EEW trained on us the whole time.

"Shoot them!" James protested. "By order of the King!"

The guard did not fire. The others did not advance.

I stared down the barrel of the conflicted man's EEW as we drew closer and saw it waver with his indecision. Stephen reached out and clasped the end of the gun. The man's grip turned weak and Stephen disarmed him with ease.

Embarrassed, the guard stood aside, and we passed through the gap between the transports. It led to the gate which controlled vehicular access onto the street which, with horror, I saw was locked.

Stephen spun round and spun me with him. "You!" he ordered the guard he had just disarmed. "Unlock the gate."

"Yes, Commander," the man spluttered.

James ran out to confront us, but Stephen raised the gun he had confiscated and aimed it at his brother.

"Stop!" he ordered.

James skidded to a halt on the grit under his feet.

"Unlike the guards, I have no compunction about shooting a royal prince if I have to," Stephen warned.

"If you do this, you will be dead to our family," said James.

"If I don't, I will be allowing our family to be the purveyors of injustice."

Behind us, I heard the clunks of locks being released on the gate.

"Then let justice be done. Let the accused stand trial."

"I can't do that. Not in that courtroom, not with that judge and not in this atmosphere of retribution."

"Then you are the one who will be called traitor and hunted as a fugitive."

The old, tired hinges of the gate squeaked as the guard opened it. I urged Stephen towards it, and this time he gave way and stepped backwards in retreat, while aiming the gun at James.

"I will find out who really killed Queen Triana, and then I shall be back. I promise you that."

Stephen turned. I broke free of his protection under the cloak and we ran out onto the street.

CHAPTER FOUR

AS SOON AS we were far enough away from the Fertillan Guard cells to be sure no one was following us, we slowed to a walk so as not to attract attention. Stephen ditched his cloak down an alley and we hurried, trying to look like we weren't hurrying, through the streets. Even though the Regellan brothers were probably the most recognisable people on the planet, no one expected a prince to be out among the general populace and nobody gave him a second look.

"Where are we going?" I asked as we headed down a street which led towards the centre of Londos.

"Somewhere we can hide out," said Stephen.

"Shouldn't we be trying to get off the planet?"

"James will have all the spaceports locked down before we can get there. I would in his position."

"Then let's go to Freddi's old farm. His daughters will take us in."

"James knows about Freddi, it wouldn't be safe – not for us, or for them."

So, despite my nervousness, I kept close to him as we bypassed the most populated area of the city to a row of service shops, all of which were closed with the lights off. Signs written high up on the buildings declared them to be a doctor's surgery, a pharmacy, a citizen's advice centre and a dental practice/hospital on the far end.

Stephen stopped at the dental practice and peered through the frosted window. "It's too late for anyone to be here. Probably just as well."

"You want us to hide out in a dentist's?"

"Not exactly," he said. "It's difficult to explain."

I looked again at the facade. It definitely looked like a dental surgery to me. A poster in the window declared a list of treatments for people with toothache, from extraction to fillings and offered minor surgery on site 'by appointment'. I shivered at the very thought of it all. I'd been through some terrifying ordeals in space, but somehow sitting voluntarily in a chair while someone in a surgical mask drilled into my teeth sounded like torture. The only other feature of the building was the door which was a multiple lock security door controlled by a combination pad at the side. Stephen tapped a series of numbers on the keypad, which I couldn't quite see, and the locks disengaged with a series of clunks. He pushed the door open and went inside.

I followed, half expecting to see some sort of secret Fertillan Guard base. But, in the dim glow of the evening's subdued light through the frosted window, I saw only what I would expect from a dentist's waiting room. A receptionist's desk was directly ahead of us, with a semi-circle of chairs laid out for waiting patients.

A lingering smell of minty disinfectant reminded me of my one and only visit to a dentist many years previously, after which I had vowed to take good care of my teeth so I didn't have to visit one ever again.

Stephen headed towards an internal door next to the reception desk. Behind it was a set of stairs leading up to the next floor where, according to the sign, I would find surgeries two to five. A door to the right was labelled Surgery One and the one on the left said it was a store cupboard.

Stephen tried the handle of the store cupboard, but it didn't budge.

"Drakh!" he muttered.

"What's in there?" I asked.

"Our hideout," he said, simply. He pulled from his pocket the EEW he had confiscated from the guard and aimed it to the right of the door handle. A burst of energy ripped through the door to create a hole the size of the beam and the handle sagged into it.

Stephen pushed at the handle and winced at the touch of blistering hot metal. The handle was dislodged, but not enough to release the door.

"Let me." I pulled my shirt sleeve down over my fingers and pushed the handle – now cooled a little – to make a hole big enough to reach through. I fumbled inside until I found the mechanism which secured the single bolt holding the door closed, and pulled it back.

Stephen kicked at the door with his boot and it swung open to reveal a small, dark room with a large hole in the back wall. It was the size of two people standing side by side and as black as space.

35

"I think this room has a manual – ah yes!" Stephen reached beside the doorframe and flicked a switch which turned on a single overhead light.

I blinked in the brightness to see the chasm at the back was surrounded by the jagged remnants of plasterboard and studwork as if someone had broken through with a hammer. Beyond that, a set of stairs led down to some sort of basement.

"The people who run the dental surgery found it by accident when they wanted to put up some shelves on the back wall of the store cupboard," Stephen explained. "When they started to drill in, they realised it wasn't a structural wall and they were concerned someone had boarded up something behind it. They thought it might have been from the time of the plague. By all accounts, this place was turned into some sort of emergency hospital back then and there was a fear it might contain bodies."

I shivered at the thought. I had been born at the time of the plague and carried the antibodies that made me immune from the virus, but I still didn't want to hide out in a chamber full of dead people.

"Don't worry," said Stephen. "We didn't find any bodies. This place was boarded up long before the plague."

"Then what is it?"

"It's easier if I show you."

Stephen closed the door behind us, as much as it was possible to do with a broken handle, and led me down the stairs.

"You're enjoying this, aren't you?" I said.

"Just a little bit."

The stairwell still had the musty smell of long-abandoned buildings and, as I walked down, running my fingers along the smooth evi-plastic walls, I was aware I was descending into the planet's crust. At the bottom of the stairs was another door, but this one wasn't locked.

Stephen turned the handle and we stepped inside. Lights flickered into existence from above as they sensed our presence.

It was a laboratory. An old, messy one quite unlike the white, clean and tidy places that came to mind when I thought of laboratories. Workbenches lined up in front of us in five rows, all with computer and scientific equipment displayed along them in what looked like a haphazard collection. The sheen of newness gleamed off some of them, while other pieces looked almost ancient and battered with years of careless handling.

The whole room, despite being at least ten times bigger than my jail cell, felt claustrophobic with a ceiling so low I could reach up and touch it. Presumably, the people who built it had dug down only as far as they needed to. The walls were lined with evi-plastic which looked like it had once been white, but had yellowed with age as it absorbed whatever it was in the Fertillan soil that gave the planet its yellow hue.

"How did you know this place was here?" I asked.

Stephen reached back into the stairwell, found a switch to turn off the light in the storeroom above and closed the door behind us. "When the people who found it thought they'd stumbled across some sort of plague tomb, the Fertillan Guard were called in to secure the area. I brought Doctor Keya Sharma in as an expert on the plague to oversee the work."

The mention of my old friend was so surprising, I had to check if I'd heard correctly. "Keya? She's here? She's okay?"

Stephen nodded. "She made sure everything was sealed off and gave inoculations to the terrified people who first stumbled across the boarded-up entrance, then we broke through. It was soon clear it had nothing to do with the plague, but it was Keya who realised what it actually was."

I looked around. It was fairly obvious to me. "It's a laboratory."

"It's the secret laboratory where scientists were carrying out research into combining the native plants of Fertilla with food crops brought from SolPrime."

The room I was standing in suddenly had a new resonance. Finding a way of growing food which had the resilience of the scraggly organisms that grew on the planet's surface had been a holy grail of Fertillan scientists ever since humans landed on the planet. It was, according to the lessons I was made to sit through in school, an impossible task because the two forms of life were too alien to each other. But my teachers had lied. The lessons were part of the deception that made sure Fertilla maintained its control over the food supply in that part of the Obsidian Rim. A group of scientists had made the breakthrough in technology, but the knowledge had been suppressed and their work destroyed.

"She found the research here?"

Stephen shrugged. "That, I don't know. I've been busy in recent months – with the wedding and everything – so I left Keya to run the place. It was badly smashed up when we found it. More or less everything was destroyed. In fact, if I hadn't brought in Keya to supervise the operation, I don't think we would ever have known what it really was."

I looked around the lab again and began to understand its contradictions. Old equipment rescued from the debris of abandoned research, mixed with new equipment brought in to continue the science. All of which had nothing to do with why I was standing there.

"We're going to hide out here?"

"No one knows about this place," said Stephen. "Apart from Keya and her staff. Most of the people who come to the dental surgery walk past it thinking it's a store cupboard and the few who know that Keya is working down here think she's an archaeologist documenting what we found. Even the guards who were on duty when we broke through were told we had found nothing and sealed it back up again. We'll be okay here for a while."

He pulled his P-tab out from his pocket and turned on the screen.

Instinctively, I grabbed it from him.

"Cassy!"

I dropped it to the floor and stamped hard on it with my boot. When I took my foot away, the P-tab was a collection of broken pieces. "They can trace the signal," I said. "You can't use that in here."

Stephen bent down and picked up what was left of the device. He dropped it onto the nearest bench and a couple of bits rolled along the surface until they hit a piece of old computer equipment and came to a halt. "I certainly can't use it now."

But I could tell by his face that he knew I was right.

"We should try to sleep so we're fresh to make a plan in the morning." I looked around the brightly lit and less than comfortable laboratory. "These motion sensor lights are going to be a problem. If we stop moving, they'll probably go off, but if we turn over in our sleep, they'll come back on and wake us up."

He thought about it for a moment. "Maybe we can find a blind spot."

We spent the next few minutes finding out where the sensors were and then it was trial and error moving to various places in the lab to see if there was somewhere they couldn't detect us. We eventually found a narrow strip along the side wall at the back where we could lie down.

With no bed and no blankets, we had to lie on the floor in only our clothes.

After a few minutes, the sensors didn't know where we were and the lights plunged us into darkness.

The adrenaline of escaping from jail had drained from my body and I felt so very tired. Stephen put his arms around me and drew me close to his body. He was warm and comforting, unlike the cold hard floor, and I forced myself to push away the tension of the day to soften into his embrace. His arms were strong and his masculine scent soothing and I pretended, as sleep claimed me, that he was all I needed to keep me safe.

CHAPTER FIVE

I WOKE WITH A start to the sound of clanging metal. I reached for my EEW, but only touched the cold, hard floor of the lab. Then I remembered, I had no gun. I had escaped from jail with only the clothes I was wearing.

I shivered in the chill of the room and realised the warmth of Stephen's body – that I had fallen asleep with – was missing.

There was another clang and something rolled across the floor towards my feet. It tripped the motion sensors and lights flooded down from above. I shaded my eyes with my hand until they adjusted to the light and I was able to see properly.

At my feet was the object. It looked like the corner of an old computer screen, all mangled with sharp edges from where it had been smashed off from the rest of the machine. From its trajectory, it appeared to have come from an open door at the back of the lab. By the sound of continued clanking from inside, I could only assume Stephen was doing something in there.

Still groggy from my uncomfortable sleep, I made my way to the lab's only toilet. When I came out, Stephen was standing outside the room and dumping an arm full of broken stuff onto a pile of junk which had suddenly appeared by the door.

"What are you doing?" I said.

"I got cold, so I went looking to see if I could find a blanket or something."

I looked down at the pile of junk. "How hidden do you think the blanket could be?"

He was about to answer when his eyes became suddenly alert and he put his finger to his lips. In the stillness of the room, I heard the distant sound of footsteps coming from the stairs.

I withdrew back into the toilet and stood behind the door while keeping it open just enough to hear what was going on.

"Hello?" a cautious female voice called out.

"Hello, Keya," said Stephen, and I relaxed to discover it was only her.

"By the Deity, Stephen!" Her voice again. "What are you doing here? Do you know half the planet is looking for you?"

I pulled open the door and stepped out into the laboratory.

Keya stood at the entrance, with the door to the stairs still open behind her. I had thought about Keya a lot in the year since I had left her back on Leontes Station. She had been exposed to the plague virus and, although she had been inoculated with the vaccine she developed, no one was sure if it had been in time to save her from a horrific death. I had often wondered if she had survived and had contemplated going back to Leontes to find out what happened. But I told myself I was too busy or couldn't afford the qubition for the journey. I didn't like to admit to myself that they were excuses because I was afraid of what I might discover.

So it was good to see her.

Her make-up was as immaculate as ever, but she had cut her long black hair so it hung in a neat bob at her shoulders. She had also dispensed with the white scientist uniform I was used to seeing her in, and was wearing a casual calf-length green skirt, matching jumper and sturdy ankle boots with a small heel. She stared at me like she couldn't quite believe I was there.

"Cassy?"

"Yeah," I said.

"They're saying you escaped from jail."

"Yeah."

Stephen went to the stairwell, turned off the light and closed the door behind her. "Can we hide out here for a while?"

Keya raised her eyebrows at him. "I presume it was you who burnt a hole in my door at the top of the stairs?"

"Sorry about that," said Stephen. "It was locked."

She frowned and pulled her P-tab from her pocket.

Stephen reached out and touched her hand to stop her. "What are you doing?"

"Telling my staff not to come in," she said. "Or do you want them all knowing that you're down here?"

Stephen pulled back his hand and allowed Keya to send her messages.

When she had finished, she replaced her P-tab in her pocket and came over to me. "Cassy, what the vac's going on?"

She unexpectedly put her arms around me and encircled me in a warm and friendly hug. I was so surprised that it took me a moment to soften into her embrace, but when I did, any doubts I had about her helping us evaporated into forgotten thoughts.

"When I heard you'd killed the Queen, I didn't believe it," said Keya.

"I didn't do it," I told her.

"Then what happened?"

I sighed and told her the whole story. From the moment the monk had come into the box at the wedding to when Stephen broke me out of jail.

"By the Deity!" she said again.

"I'm sorry we came here," said Stephen, "but I didn't know where else to go."

"Not back out into Londos," she said. "There are Fertillan Guards everywhere. I got stopped *twice* on the way here. There's a public alert out for you two and everyone I passed is talking about it."

I turned to Stephen. "We *have* to get out of Londos and off Fertilla."

"It's too dangerous," he said.

"Stephen's right," said Keya. "You'll barely get to the end of the street before being arrested."

I looked around at the four walls of the lab. It was a lot bigger than my jail cell, but I didn't feel any less incarcerated. "We can't stay here forever."

Stephen put a gentle hand on my shoulder. "The safest thing is to hide out here until the fuss has died down. The last thing we need is to make any rash moves."

"Is Freddi here?" asked Keya.

"He'll be being watched," said Stephen. "James is many things, but he's no fool."

"Freddi could still be useful as an ally on the outside," said Keya. "I'll put some feelers out. But, don't worry, I'll be subtle."

"Thanks, Keya," I said.

She shrugged it off. "In the meantime, how about I give you the tour?"

"The tour?"

"Has Stephen shown you around the lab?"

"Not really."

"Then I shall show you."

Keya stood in front of the double doors at the back of the lab. They had no handles, but a sensor-operated control pad was cut into the wall off to the right side. By the look of the fresh, white piece of evi-plastic lining around it, it had been freshly installed.

Keya placed her palm on the pad, there was a clicking behind the doors and a sigh as the airtight seal between them was broken. Motors inside slid both doors sideways into hidden pockets in the wall and revealed a small room bathed in light. An amazing smell rushed to greet us: musty and fresh like stepping into an agro-dome. As my eyes grew used to the light, which was soft and pinkish like the Fertillan sun shining through the planet's atmosphere, I saw every wall of the small room was covered floor to ceiling with racks of transparent trays filled with dirt. Most of them had the little white tendrils of roots snaking through them and some had tiny green shoots reaching up into the light.

Stepping inside and turning round to face me, Keya too was bathed in light. "Isn't it inspirational?"

"What is it?" I asked.

"A plant bank."

"These are hybrid Fertillan/SolPrime plants?"

"No," said Keya. She shook her head and smiled at the very idea. "That would have been amazing, but no. These are our base plants. Some are native Fertillan plants and others are SolPrime natives. I think, actually, the Fertillan ones are struggling to survive in the heat and the oxygen-rich atmosphere. We may have to build a second propagation chamber for them."

"Stephen said this was the lab where the food research was originally carried out. From the way he said it, I thought it might be the one where they made the breakthrough."

"That's my theory," said Keya. "Although, whoever destroyed it did a thorough job. Everything was smashed up. Sometimes to the point where you couldn't tell what bit of equipment the pieces used to belong to. This propagation chamber was a mass of dried out dirt and smashed trays. Everything was long dead. One of my staff has been trying to extract DNA from what was left, but that seems to be a waste of time – it was too badly degraded."

"So, what are you doing here?"

"When the place turned out to have nothing to do with the plague, Stephen hired me to get the lab back up and running to continue the food research."

"Does that mean some of the research survived?"

"Not really," said Keya. "Mostly we found unsalvageable junk."

"Then how? I thought the last remaining research document was destroyed."

The document was how I had first met Keya. Despite the efforts of people who wanted to bury the knowledge that the scientists had discovered, others had risked their lives to save the research. I had taken it to her in the hope a new food technology could be created to feed a growing population in the Obsidian Rim. But forces within the Fertillan Guard had found out where I had gone and had the document destroyed: in the most devastating way possible – by setting enough bombs to blow up the entire space station and taking with it many of Keya's colleagues, including her lover.

"The document was destroyed. But not before some of us were able to read it. We don't have the details, of course, but those of us who survived remember a little of what we read. The basic principles and the techniques they used are something we can recreate. Stephen said he would pay for me to work in secret down here with some trusted colleagues." She paused and lowered her eyes in thought. "I suppose that is all under threat now."

"I'm sorry, Keya."

She shrugged. "Seems to be the story of my life. I keep thinking I should take a teaching job somewhere. You know, settle down and pass the struggle onto the next generation."

An almighty clatter from outside broke the contemplative mood.

"What the–?" Keya strode straight past me and out of the propagation chamber.

I followed to see Stephen standing over the same pile of rubbish he had dumped earlier. Except the pile was now much larger and, by the look of Stephen's flushed face and dusty clothes, he had just deposited an armful of more stuff on top of it.

Keya quickly closed the doors of the plant bank and looked at him with the displeased expression of a teacher who's had her class disrupted. "What are you doing?"

He ignored the question by asking one of his own and indicating the open door behind him. "What's this room for?"

"It's a junk room," said Keya. "There were only bits and pieces stored in there when we found it, so we used it to put everything in while we were clearing up the main lab."

"It's a room full of junk, certainly. But I'm not sure that's what it's supposed to be," said Stephen. "Do you know what's behind it?"

"Behind it?" said Keya, like the question was nonsensical. "There's nothing behind it. It's the back of the lab."

"That's what I thought. Except the people here seem to have a tendency to hide things behind the back of store cupboards."

Stephen went inside. Keya exchanged a glance with me and we followed.

The room went back as far as the propagation chamber, which would suggest that was as far as the basement level extended. Piles of junk, like the piece of broken computer which had rolled towards me that morning, were stacked up on the left side, leaving most of the right side and the back wall clear.

"Can you explain why you've taken a bunch of mess which was perfectly happy being kept out of the way in here and dumped it out into my clean lab?" said Keya.

Stephen turned and looked at both of us. One to the other as if he was expecting something. "You haven't seen it, have you?"

"Seen what?" I said.

He pointed at the right side of the room where the wall met the floor. A border about five centimetres high and two centimetres thick ran along the join. Unlike the walls with their yellowed evi-plastic lining, it had remained pristine white, other than for a few dark scuff marks.

I had seen such borders before, but didn't know what they were called. "It's one of those things that nice houses have at the edge of their floors," I said. "You have them in Londos House. It's a bit odd to have one in a storeroom, I suppose."

"I thought it was a skirting board as well, at first," he said. "But it's not – the back wall doesn't have one. It's actually trunking." He pointed his finger along the line taken by the white border until it ended just before the corner where a collection of five multi-coloured cables came out of the end and curved back into the wall where they disappeared.

"So, it's trunking," I said. "So what? It keeps the cables out of the way."

But Keya was staring at the corner where the cables were visible. "By the Deity," she said under her breath.

"What?" I looked between both of them, getting frustrated that no one was telling me anything.

"If it's a solid wall at the back of this room," said Stephen. "Then where do the cables go?"

It was so obvious when he said it that I was embarrassed at not realising what he was talking about from the beginning. But trunking was so ubiquitous across the Rim, including inside my spaceship, that it seemed perfectly normal. What was rare on Fertilla were rooms built into the crust of the planet. Utility wires, cables and ducts would often be hidden underground, but in shallow, accessible passageways in the street, not at the bottom of a basement of a dental surgery.

If there really were cables running along the wall, it made no sense for them to disappear into a solid wall. Unless it wasn't a solid wall at all.

"By the Deity," I said, echoing Keya's astonishment. "There's another room hidden behind that wall."

CHAPTER SIX

WE ALL STOOD and stared at the blank wall.

"We should get a hammer and knock it down," said Stephen.

"We have no idea what's behind there," I pointed out. "It could be anything. It could be a pit of plague victims."

"Unlikely," said Keya. "This lab dates from years before the outbreak and was sealed up tight. Whoever built this wall must have done so before the lab was smashed up and closed down."

"Then maybe the scientists hid their research in there," said Stephen.

"Assuming this really is a false wall." Keya ran her hand along the smooth surface until she reached the middle where she knocked at it with her fist. It answered with a dull thud. "Sounds solid enough. But it's hard to tell with the evi-plastic layer."

She turned and walked out of the room.

"Where are you going?" Stephen called after her.

51

"To find that hammer you asked for."

I listened to her shoes *tap tap* on the floor as she walked across the lab and then the sound of her footsteps receding up the stairs.

"Should we even be doing this?" I asked Stephen.

"Don't you want to know what's behind there?" he replied.

"Not really. There's only two reasons someone hides something behind a wall: to protect whatever it is they've hidden from other people; or to protect people from whatever it is they've hidden. We've got bigger things to worry about."

"We're stuck here until things cool down a bit," he said. "This will keep our mind off it."

"I don't want to keep my mind off it. I want to keep my mind sharp. We need a plan to get out of here, Stephen. All our energies should be focussed on that. You weren't the one dragged in handcuffs through a crowd of people baying for your blood. You've spent all your life wrapped in the privileged cocoon of being a prince, you don't understand what it's like to be an ordinary person not in control of everything around you."

"But you heard what James said, by breaking you out of jail, I am as much a fugitive as you are."

"That's what I mean," I said. "You can't stand here and pretend everything is going to be okay because, out in the real world where you're not treated like a prince, everything *isn't* okay."

"Cassy…"

He came towards me and reached out for my shoulder as if to comfort me, but I shook him off. "We need a *plan*, Stephen. We can't hide out here forever."

The sound of Keya's returning footsteps stopped us saying anything more.

She came back into the room and gave us both a look which suggested she sensed the tension between us, but she opted to say nothing. She had with her a small power tool which she lifted to show us. It was a drill, with a grip small enough to fit comfortably in her hand and a drill bit sticking out of the top that was so thin it looked like it would snap under very little pressure.

"That doesn't look much like a hammer," I observed.

"It's a dentist's drill," she said. "An old one that was due to go for recycling. I thought we could use it to drill through the wall. If we hit rock, we'll know there isn't another room behind there. If we hit air, we can make the hole bigger and see what's on the other side."

Stephen took it from her and turned it in his hand. "Doesn't look strong enough."

"It's diamond tipped for drilling into teeth," she said. "It should do the job."

Stephen must have found the button that operated it because a motor whirred and the drill bit spun in a blur.

He stopped it and pressed it to the evi-plastic. The motor whirred once again, but the bit slipped off the smooth surface and spun noisily as it drilled into air. Stephen stopped it, put it back on the same spot and tried again. A thin curl of the membrane spiralled off the drill as the diamond tip ate into the evi-plastic. The noise of the motor changed and sounded hungrier as it struck whatever was beneath.

"Stop!" I called, as something in the corner of the room caught my eye. At first, I had thought the dark line where the two walls met was an effect of the light. But the closer I looked, the more it appeared to be a join in the evi-plastic.

"What is it?" Stephen allowed the drill to fall silent and took it away from the wall where it had barely made a pinprick.

"Give me that." I gestured for him to hand over the drill.

Its fine, diamond-tipped point was perfect for picking at the join.

"What are you doing?" he said.

"Everywhere in the lab, the lining of the walls is one continuous sheet. If there are joins anywhere, then they are moulded invisibly into the next section. Except here."

I managed to get the drill bit under the tiniest flap of evi-plastic. I teased it back and the drill slipped. I forced it under the flap a second time and pushed harder. The drill bit snapped in half. I stumbled backwards with the sudden release and the broken end of the drill pinged onto the floor.

"Well, that's not helpful," complained Stephen.

I ignored him. The flap was now big enough to grasp with my thumb and forefinger. Putting the drill down, I grabbed the loose bit of evi-plastic. The glue that had stuck it down was old, decayed and started to give way. As I peeled away the top yellowed layer, it revealed a pristine white surface underneath.

Keya stepped in to help pull at the flap. A rasping, tearing sound accompanied each tug until half the wall was exposed. It also revealed the corner of a large rectangular crack set into the centre. It began above our heads and ran down in a straight line to beneath the rest of the yellowed outer layer. Stephen joined in and, with one final yank, the rest of the evi-plastic sheet came off in one go.

We found ourselves looking at a white wall, not tinged yellow by years of absorbing the colour of Fertilla's rock. There were blobs of grey, decaying glue all over it where someone had covered it up with an evi-plastic disguise and, in the centre, was a geometric fissure in the shape of a doorway.

But if it was a door, it was one without a handle, without any hinges and with no control panel to open it.

"How do we get in?" asked Stephen.

"I've seen these sort of doors before," said Keya. "There's usually a hidden panel." She ran her hand down the wall to the left of the door. "There." She pressed her palm into the wall and an unseen mechanism clanked as it lurched into action.

Keya backed away. The door clicked and hissed as the whole thing eased backwards from the wall on automatic arms and slid sideways to reveal a rectangular opening into blackness. The ambient light from the storeroom only seeped in enough to reveal the dark outlines of several large objects at waist height.

We looked at each other, as we all silently wondered if it was safe to go in. Stephen pulled out his EEW and took the first step.

Lights flickered on and Stephen's figure became a silhouette in the doorway. Nothing else happened. He didn't move, he didn't fire his gun.

"Is it safe?" I called out.

"Yeah, I think so." He paused, as if uncertain. "Everyone's dead."

My body gave an involuntary shiver. The dead were the safest people to encounter. They wouldn't attack you, they wouldn't hurt you, they wouldn't lie to you. Even so, my instinct warned me to be wary.

Keya gave me a questioning glance. "Shall we?"

Together, we stepped in.

I prepared myself to see the remains of bodies stacked up inside, like in an overwhelmed and abandoned mortuary.

Instead, I found myself stepping into another laboratory. It was long and thin, the same width as the storeroom, and half the length of the main lab. Down each side, raised on benches, were human-sized pods, like coffins with glass lids. There were six of them, all with cables trailing out of the back which were plugged into a junction box inside the door. The box had to be what was connected to the cables Stephen had seen coming out of the trunking.

Stephen stood beside the nearest pod and stared down through the lid. I joined him.

"By the Deity," I whispered, as I looked into the long-dead face of what must have once been a woman. Her wrinkled, leathery skin had sunk down to her skull and left the grimacing smile of her teeth exposed between her desiccated lips. Her hair, which might have once been luscious brown, appeared wiry and brittle resting on the soft mound of a pillow under her head. She wore clothes, but these had also collapsed down onto her skeleton as the moisture from her flesh had evaporated away so she looked like she was dressed in trousers and shirt two sizes too big for her. At the end of her shirt cuffs were two withered hands that had dried to the point where it was possible to see the individual bones underneath her skin.

Stephen swallowed hard. "Do you know what it is?"

"It's a cryo-pod," I said.

"That's what I thought."

"I saw them in the museum on a school history trip when I was little. I didn't think they would work any more."

"It seems they didn't," said Stephen.

In the early days of humanity's colonisation of the galaxy, people would be put into the pods to hibernate while ships travelled the vast distances of space in the hope of finding new worlds where they could live. People could survive, it was said, the equivalent of many generations before being woken up to start their new life. Even when wormhole technology allowed us to move around the galaxy in the relative blink of an eye, pioneers still used the pods in order for a small team to set up a habitat before waking up the rest of their passengers. Fertilla was colonised like that. Or so I was taught.

I turned away from the woman's desiccated body and was faced with yet another failed pod on the other side of the narrow room. Its occupant, by the looks of him, was a man. Almost wasted away like the woman: shut up and forgotten about for years behind the wall of a storeroom.

"Why did they do it?" I said. "Why go into cryo-sleep on an already colonised planet?"

"And why hide them away down here?" said Stephen.

Keya called out from the far end of the room. "This one's still alive!"

"What?!"

I broke away from Stephen and rushed to where Keya was staring down into one of the pods.

I stared too. The face of a young woman, plump with the presence of flesh and muscle beneath her soft brown skin, rested peacefully on the pillow of her pod with her eyes closed. Like she was asleep.

Stephen joined me at my shoulder. "I guess we can ask her those questions," he said.

"Keya can," I said. "We still need to work out a plan to get off Fertilla without being arrested and executed."

Stephen pointed at a display panel on the side of the pod. "What do those numbers mean?"

There were six numbers in three pairs of two: *05:02:45*. As I watched, the last pair of numbers became *44* and then *43*.

"They indicate the cryogenic revival sequence," said Keya.

I glared at her.

She was unfazed. "You don't expect me to leave her like this, do you?"

"Well, no…" I said. "But she's been down here for years, a few more days won't do her any harm."

"It's too late," said Keya. "I've started the sequence. It can't be stopped."

"What does that mean?" asked Stephen.

"It means," she said. "That in just over five hours and two minutes, this sleeping woman is going to wake up."

CHAPTER SEVEN

WE TOOK IT in turns to watch the sleeping woman.

Nothing appeared to change. She remained unanimated, resting on the soft pillow of her cryo-pod with her eyes closed and the machinery keeping her body on the edge of death. But, somewhere within the pod, the systems silently brought her closer to life. They increased the pumping of her heart, they stimulated her lungs to take in oxygen and revived her brain to the point where it would resume control of her bodily functions. Slowly, so we could not see it, but definitively, so her body would experience a return to consciousness.

Sitting cross-legged on the floor next to her was an unnerving experience. I felt like a medium at a seance, forming the bridge between the world of the living and the world of the dead. Behind me, lying where I dare not look inside the other pods, remained the bodies of the five who had not survived. Keya thought the pods were originals from the first colonisation of Fertilla which had malfunctioned in some way. Either that, or a power failure had interrupted their life-support systems long enough to prove fatal. Only one of the pods at the back had pulled through, possibly because it was at the end of the chain of resources and, by luck or judgement, pulled enough power from the backup systems to allow its inhabitant to survive.

The countdown clicked into its final hour.

The woman's chest rose and fell with a shallow breath.

"Keya!"

I scrambled to my feet and placed my hands on the glass lid of the pod to feel the faint vibration of power within. The woman's face was still and serene under the transparent barrier with neither her lips nor her nostrils reacting to the passage of air.

Keya came running. "What is it?"

"She breathed!" I said. Although, looking at her inanimate body lying there, I began to doubt myself. "I think."

Keya glanced at the countdown. "We're in the final hour. It's entirely possible. This is the point where her life hangs in the balance."

"But she's alive. She survived," I said.

"She survived until this point. Waking from cryo-sleep puts a lot of strain on the body. Sometimes people would lie dormant for generations on the old colonisation ships, only to slip away in the final moments before they were about to start their new life."

Stephen joined us. "Is she waking up?"

"Not long now," said Keya.

So all three of us took the last shift of the watch. After ten minutes, I saw the woman breathe again. This time, Keya and Stephen saw it too. Ten minutes later, her hand twitched.

Another ten minutes and she let out a tiny groan, like a person in the middle of a dream.

The countdown reached the final ten minutes.

Her eyelids flickered. She gasped for breath like someone pulled into a spaceship from the vacuum and suddenly tried to sit up. She struck her forehead on the inside of the lid and collapsed back down on the pillow again.

The display said she still had eight minutes to go.

"She's waking too soon!" said Keya.

"Is that bad?" I said.

"Yes," said Keya. "I mean, I think so."

"Shouldn't eight minutes mean eight minutes?" said Stephen.

Keya shrugged. "I've never done this before. I work in a lab with microscopes and Petri dishes, not with people."

The woman's eyes snapped open and the light sent her large, black pupils shrinking into the brown of her irises. She reached up to the glass lid and pressed her palms on it so hard that blood receded from her skin with the pressure. Her face became full of panic and she banged on the glass.

"We need to get her out!" I looked around the outside of the pod for some sort of control which would open it.

"Stephen's right," said Keya. "We should wait the eight minutes."

"If you woke up in a glass coffin, would you want to be kept trapped in there for eight minutes? The shock will kill her!"

Keya stared at the countdown as it ticked down to: *00:07:59.* "For the Deity's sake, I hope you're right, Cassy."

She tapped something out on the panel and locks clicked open all around the perimeter of the pod. The woman's battering hands dislodged the lid, but she didn't have the strength to get it off of her.

I pushed it back and the lid went flying off, hit the wall behind and fell to the floor.

The woman cried out in a silent scream. Then she opened and closed her mouth over and over like a newly hatched bird demanding food from its parents.

"It's okay, it's okay," I said in the most soothing voice I could manage.

I don't know if she understood me because her eyes stared – unseeing – straight past me. She tried to sit up again, but her body was too weak and she flopped back down on the pillow.

I leant in and cradled her like a baby, but she resisted me as best she could in her weakened state and beat her fists down on my back.

"Okay, okay," I kept saying as I held onto her fragile, skeletal body. "You're alive. You're awake. It's okay."

She stopped fighting me and, for a moment, I thought she had passed out. But as I pulled back and held her at arm's length, I saw she was still conscious. She looked around her environment with what appeared to be focussing eyes. She squinted at my face like she was trying to understand its shape, or maybe trying to work out if she recognised me. She opened her mouth again, and this time a sound came out. Not a word, but a moan. Like a guttural noise from a child who hasn't yet learnt how to speak.

I put my palm to my chest. "My name's Cassy. What's your name?"

"Mmm. Mmm," was all she said.

"Don't rush her," said Keya.

Panic gripped her again and she grabbed hold of the edge of her pod. She pressed down on it and her legs kicked like she was trying to get out.

"Take it easy," I said.

But my words only made her more anxious. "Mmm! Mmm!" She leant onto the edge of the pod with all her body weight and thrashed her legs. It was enough to topple her over and she would have fallen to the ground if Stephen hadn't stepped in to catch her.

"She should stay in the pod until she's recovered," said Keya.

"I don't think she wants to," I said.

Stephen lowered the woman's legs so her feet touched the floor. He attempted to let them take a little of her own weight, but her legs buckled and he had to catch her again.

"I need to get someone." Keya turned and rushed out of the room.

"Get who?" I called after her.

"Don't worry, we can trust him!" And she was gone.

Stephen manoeuvred the woman to a seated position. Her head flopped to the side from weak neck muscles that hadn't been used for years and I sat next to her so she could rest her head on me.

She opened and closed her mouth again as if to speak. The only things that came out were breaths.

"Stephen, go and find her a glass of water, will you?"

"Are you sure you're going to be okay?"

I nodded.

But as soon as he had left the room, the woman started shaking. I took off my jacket and placed it around her shoulders to keep her warm. But she kept shaking and I feared she was going into shock.

Stephen returned and stood before us with a mug in his hand. He looked worried.

"Well, don't just stand there, give it to me!"

Stephen passed the mug and I held it to the woman's lips, but her instinct to drink hadn't returned and when I tipped it up, the water spilled out and dribbled down her shirt.

I took the mug away and her tongue came out to lick the moisture left on her face. It gave me an idea and I put my finger into the water and dabbed it on her lips. Something lit up behind her eyes – a spark of understanding. "Mmm! Mmm!"

"More?"

I couldn't hold much water on my finger and so I pulled my shirt sleeve down below my hand and dipped the end in the mug to moisten it. I touched the fabric to her lips. She seemed to understand what I was doing and allowed me to push the material into her mouth. Her instinct to suck, which all children are born with, took over and she began taking in fluid.

At that point, I heard footsteps at the door and turned to see Keya had brought a man with her. He was bearded with a full head of dark hair peppered with grey and he was tall, at least one head height taller than Stephen and considerably taller than Keya. He wore a white tunic like a scientist and carried a plump medical bag in one hand.

He looked around the room with astonishment. "What the vac is this place, Keya?"

"Are you a doctor?" I asked him.

"I'm a dentist," he said. "But to qualify, I had to take a certain amount of medical training."

"More training than me." I moved aside so he had full view of the woman who had been woken from cryo-sleep.

He rushed to her and knelt on the floor.

He felt her wrist for a pulse.

"Is she going to be okay?" I asked.

"I'm not sure," he said.

CHAPTER EIGHT

T HE DENTIST STABILISED the woman's condition over the course of an anxious hour.

It was the administering of a saline solution to deliver fluid into her bloodstream which seemed to have the most effect. It stopped her shivering and calmed her pulse. He retrieved some bedding supplies from up in the dental surgery and made somewhere semi-comfortable for her to lie down on the floor of the cryo-chamber where she fell into a normal sleep. He watched her for many minutes while she breathed out, breathed gently in, and breathed out again.

When he stood up from her side and turned towards us, I could tell by his expression that the immediate danger was over. "You should watch over her for the next couple of days," he said. "The effects of the cryo-sleep will still be in her body. There's a chance she could relapse."

"Thank you, doctor," I said. "I'm sorry, in all the rush I didn't ask your name."

"Robbi Harrist," he said. "My friends call me Rob."

"Are we your friends?" I asked him.

He looked at Keya as he pondered my question. "You are Keya's friends."

Stephen held out his hand for the dentist to shake. "Thank you, Doctor Harrist. I'm–"

"I know who you are," he retorted. He made no move to shake Stephen's hand and Stephen had to withdraw it so his arm hung back down, rejected, by his side. "I don't know what I should be more surprised by: having a woman wake from cryo-sleep in the basement I didn't know I had, or having Prince Stephen Regellan and the assassin he helped escape from jail hiding out down here."

I shot a concerned glance at Stephen.

Stephen looked the dentist directly in the eye. "I hope I can rely on your discretion," said Stephen.

"Of course, Your Highness," said Rob, bowing his head in a feigned nod of respect. "I have promised Keya."

With that, he left the cryo-chamber. Keya followed close behind him and we brought up the rear. But, at the entrance to the storeroom, I tugged at Stephen's sleeve to hold him back. From the doorway, we watched as Keya walked with him to the front of the lab. There, they spoke together in hushed tones.

"Do you think we can trust him?" I asked Stephen.

"I think we're going to have to," he said.

Doctor Robbi Harrist bent down to give Keya a quick kiss on the lips.

He then walked up the stairs towards the dental surgery.

She must have known what we were talking about because when Keya came back, she gave us a superior look. "I had to bring him down here. That woman could have died."

"I'm not questioning your decision," said Stephen. "It's just the more people who know we're here, the more risky it is. For us and for him."

A woman's cry erupted from the chamber. It was hoarse and rasping from a voice which had been dormant for many years. But, as she cried out again, it turned into a loud and terrified scream.

We rushed into the cryo-chamber to see the woman had got to her feet and, somehow, walked across the room to the pod opposite hers with the saline drip still plugged into her arm and the bag pulled off the hook it was hanging on so it dragged on the floor behind her. She slapped her hands on the clear glass, opened her mouth wide and let out a piercing scream. She must have seen the desiccated remains of the man who was sealed inside.

I cradled her fragile body and tried to pull her away, but she had surprising strength and resisted.

"No!" she said. The first word she had spoken.

"Come away from there," I said, gently pulling her towards me. "Come and sit down."

"No," she said again. She put her nose close to the glass and looked at the long-dead face of the man she must have known. "No, no, no!"

Her cries turned to tears as the saline Doctor Harrist had put into her body gave her enough fluids to cry. "Come on," I said. This time, she allowed me to take her weight and guide her back to the makeshift bed which we had constructed on the floor. She collapsed onto it. I sat on the floor next to her and her head flopped onto my shoulder where she sobbed uncontrollably until there was a damp patch on my shirt.

Stephen and Keya stood over us anxiously, until I told them to give the poor woman some space and they reluctantly moved to the other side of the chamber where they sat and watched.

After many minutes, she seemed to run out of moisture and emotion and her sobbing subsided. She lifted up her head from my shoulder to reveal a red and tear-stained face. Like the face of any normal grieving person. I took that as a good sign.

She looked directly at me. There was a question in her eyes which she seemed unable to articulate. "Wha-? Wha-?"

"What happened?" I suggested.

She nodded.

"We're not sure," I said. "The other pods failed."

"Only... only me?"

"Yes, you're the only one who survived. The others died in cryo-sleep. I'm sorry."

She threw her head back in despair and it hit the wall behind her. So much was her shock and grief that she seemed not to notice.

She looked at me again. "Eden?"

"They all died," I repeated.

"No, *Eden!*"

"I don't which one was Eden, I'm sorry."

She got exasperated and waved her hands around. The saline line, which was still plugged into her vein, flapped in front of her face.

Keya left her position where she was watching and came over. "There'll be plenty of time for talking later. You should rest now."

Keya put her hands on the woman's shoulders and tried to lay her down, but the woman pushed back. "No! Want to… *need* to know."

"Okay." Keya let go. "But take your time. There's no rush."

The woman nodded. She swallowed hard as if to prepare herself. "You don't know about Eden?"

"No," said Keya.

"We found you by accident," I told her. "We don't know who you are or why you were here. Perhaps you could start from the beginning. Maybe by telling us your name. My name is Cassy."

"Theressi," said the woman. "Terri for short. People call me Terri."

"Nice to meet you, Terri," I said. "This is Keya and Stephen."

The two others completed their introductions with a smile and a nod. I could feel the tension as we all waited for the woman – Terri – to tell us her story. I tried not to appear eager, but I wasn't entirely sure I succeeded.

"If I tell you," said Terri. "You won't kill me?"

"No!" I said. "Why would we do that?"

"Because it's blasphemy."

Keya leant forward. "Are you something to do with the laboratory that was hidden down here? I've been trying to recreate their work."

Terri reached out and grabbed her hand. "You're a scientist?"

She looked so excited, I became worried about the effect on her fragile body.

"The beginning," I reminded her.

She took a couple of breaths to calm herself. "My family are – were – also scientists. They were bio… bio…"

She struggled over the word, then smiled as she seemed to decide it didn't matter. "My mother studied Fertillan plants and how they were able to survive on a planet which was so hostile to life. My father worked on the food crops humans brought out to the Rim. Everyone said the two genotypes couldn't be combined, but no one had tried since the early days of colonisation. My father decided to re-open the research. He said success was easier than all the old texts said it would be, but I think he was more brilliant than he liked to admit. My family employed more staff, I came back from my studies to join them. But what we found scared a lot of people."

Terri looked down in her lap where her bony fingers clasped each other. She paused, like the memory was too painful.

Keya gave her an encouraging smile. "We know the lab was hidden down here for a reason."

Terri nodded. "We feared for the research, we feared for our lives. My parents wrote up what they had learnt in a document in the hope that someone in the future could continue what we had been doing. That's when the purges started and that's when people died.

"We knew we couldn't stay on Fertilla and so my parents found an old colony ship – at least, they hired someone to find one for them. They filled it with all their research, the hybrid plants and everything they had. They called it Eden. They were going to develop new ecosystems on that ship, like the ecosystems that sustained the earlier pioneers on their journey, but these would mimic the harsher environments found on other planets in the Obsidian Rim where they would grow hybrids bred to survive under extreme conditions. We were going to create a whole new community there. But someone sold us out. The kill squads were sent out when we tried to get to Eden. We had to abandon our plan and come back here while the others on the ship left without us."

"But why go into cryo-sleep?" said Keya.

"If we tried to leave Fertilla, we were dead," said Terri. "If we stayed on Fertilla, we were dead. The only other option was to hide. The cryo-pods had been taken off the old ship and brought here for study. Paulus thought he could make them work again." She glanced up at the pod where she had seen the body of the dead man and I presumed he was the man she was speaking of. "It was never his intention for us to use them. Until we had no other option."

"Then the people in the pods are your parents and some of the other scientists?" I said.

"Yes," she said. "We thought, when the Eden ship was successful and returned to Fertilla, no one would be able to doubt the science that we were trying to prove. We could be revived into a time when people valued our work and no one would try to kill us for it."

"I'm afraid the time never came," said Keya. "The lab was smashed up and shut away. It was only by chance that we discovered it was here. The people who sealed you up in the cryo-chamber probably died taking your secret with them."

"How long...?" said Terri.

"I don't know how long you were in cryo-sleep," said Keya. "It could be as much as a hundred years."

"A hundred years to advance and no one did anything?"

"I wouldn't say nobody did anything. Some of us–"

"I want to see the lab," Terri interrupted.

"I think you should rest," said Keya.

"I want to see it!"

Terri pushed herself to her feet, despite Keya's attempts to stop her, and swayed unsteadily. She seemed determined and so we helped her – with each of us holding onto her arms on each side – through the door of the chamber, into the storeroom with its remnants of junk, and out into the laboratory.

We steered her towards the nearest stool and she perched on it while she leant onto the bench in front of her and looked around.

"It looks so different," she said.

"It was a mess when we came in," said Keya. "We tidied up and brought in new equipment so we can start again."

She stared, wide-eyed at Keya. "Start again? Nothing survived?"

"I was able to read the document before it was destroyed," said Keya. "But nothing was left in the lab apart from a lot of broken equipment. And you. *You* survived. Perhaps you can teach me the knowledge that was lost."

Terri's stare softened as the tears came to her eyes again. "My parents led the research. I was just their assistant, I hadn't long returned from my studies."

Her tears turned to weeping and her head collapsed onto Keya's shoulder. "That's enough for today," she said, stroking Terri's hair to soothe her. "Let's take you back."

I helped carry her, as she could barely walk, back to the chamber where we laid her in the makeshift bed and let her fall back to sleep again. This time, she was exhausted enough to stay there for eight, uninterrupted hours.

CHAPTER NINE

AT THE SOUND of footsteps on the stairwell, Stephen grabbed my arm and pulled me back into the storeroom. He took his EEW from his pocket and held it up at his shoulder; ready to fire if he needed to.

Terri must have heard something was going on and came running out of the cryo-chamber. She opened her mouth to say something, but I put my finger to my lips. She stopped like a statue and stared at us as we listened at the closed door.

Two people had come into the lab and I heard the soft mumble of women's voices.

One of them called out: "Cassy?"

The voice wasn't Keya's, but it sounded familiar. I reached out for the door handle, but Stephen's hand got there first and stopped me. His look told me not to go out there, but I pushed his hand away. Even if the person was hostile, they obviously knew I was there and I decided I would rather go out to face them than let them come in to face us.

I crept, tentatively, into the lab.

Keya was standing by the door with another woman who was slightly taller than she was. The woman was thin and athletic with soft curls of ginger-red hair that fell to her shoulder blades. Seeing her allowed me to place where I had heard her voice before – at Freddi's old farm. She was one of Freddi's daughters.

As soon as she saw me, she came rushing over. "Cassy, you're alive!" she said and grabbed my shoulders as if to check it was true.

"Yes," I said. "Shouldn't I be?"

"People are saying you haven't been caught so you must be dead."

"No, thankfully."

Stephen emerged from the storeroom. After a moment, he pocketed his EEW.

Her mouth fell open when she saw him. "Prince Stephen!" She curtsied low.

He took her reverence in his stride. "I'm afraid you have me at a disadvantage."

"I'm Angelina Aaron, Your Highness," she said, with another quick curtsy. "You know my father, Frederus Aaron."

"Ah, you are Freddi's daughter." He nodded. "I see the family resemblance."

I was glad he had asked the question. Freddi had two daughters and, every time I met them, I had to be reminded which one was Jan and which one was Ange. Ange was the older of the two, a good ten years older than me, and still strikingly beautiful with a tough, darkened quality to her skin that I had only seen among farmers.

"How did you get here?" I asked.

"The transports are up and running again," said Ange. "They couldn't keep Londos locked down forever."

"I meant, how did you find us?"

Keya walked towards us from the back of the room. "I put out feelers, as I said I would," she said. "Don't worry, I was subtle."

"One of the labourers who works on the farm brought a message," Ange explained. "It said I had an urgent dental appointment in town. I knew it was some kind of code because I've never had a dental appointment in my life. That's how I came to meet Keya."

"Have you seen Freddi? Is he okay?" I asked.

Her smile faded and her face seemed to lose some of its healthy glow. "He's been arrested. The Fertillan Guard came to our farm and marched him away. I haven't been able to speak to him. It's been *days* now."

Moisture formed in her eyes, but she blinked it away as she held back the emotion.

"Here," said Keya, taking her arm. "Come and sit down."

She led Ange to a stool beside one of the benches.

"They must know he didn't have anything to do with the assassination," I said. "He was in the main hall – there were hundreds of witnesses."

"I don't think they care," said Ange. "They can't arrest you, so they arrested him."

Stephen came over to reassure her. "Don't worry. He's done nothing wrong. He will be questioned and released."

Ange glared at him. "Are you sure about that? You didn't see the way they dragged him away."

"They want us, not him," said Stephen. "Once we escape, they'll have to let him go."

"I hope you're right," said Ange. "Which is why I'm here. Before Dad was arrested, he gave me details of someone who might be able to smuggle you off Fertilla. If you made contact, I was to make the arrangements while the Fertillan Guard were watching him." She paused. "But he said you won't like it."

"Why would he say that?" I asked.

"He said, when you met Patti before, you two didn't exactly get on."

"Patti." The name gave me a chill.

"Dad said she has experience in smuggling people off planets."

"Oh yeah," I said. "She has experience all right."

"Who's Patti?" asked Keya.

"A people trafficker – last time I travelled with her, she was taking people to die in medical experiments."

"Don't be so harsh," said Stephen. "She didn't know that's what was happening to them. Remember, she helped us stop a deadly virus being released on Manupia."

"Only because you were paying her," I retorted.

"Dad said you would react like that." Ange smiled. "But he said she could be trusted and I believe him. I don't see how else you're going to get out of here. There are Fertillan Guards everywhere, they've set up checkpoints at the transport hubs, they've set up checkpoints in the street. Everything going out of Londos is scrutinised and everything going through the spaceport has to be signed off. They're checking people, cargo – everything. You're going to need specialist help to get off the planet."

"I don't know." I looked to Stephen. "What do you think?"

He let out a slow, thoughtful breath. "There is a limit to how long we can hide out down here."

"I agree, but jumping out of the frying pan and into the fire wasn't what I had in mind."

"Perhaps we should reserve judgement until Angelina has told us Patti's plan," he said. "Patti has a plan, I presume?"

"Yes," said Ange. "But that's the other thing you're not going to like. To get off Fertilla, you have to be dead."

CHAPTER TEN

N O ONE CHECKS on dead bodies, was the theory.

People were checked, vehicles were checked, cargo was checked. But dead bodies? They were dead. Who wanted to open a stranger's coffin and be reminded of their own mortality? Not a member of the Fertillan Guard bored out of their head after many days monitoring out-going shipments. Or so went the theory.

On Fertilla, the dead were burnt in a funeral cremation ceremony and their ashes recycled, but it wasn't unusual for off-worlders to want to go back to their colony of origin once they died. The rich would have the resources to pay for them to be transported home for a funeral befitting of their culture which all their friends and relatives could attend. If Stephen and I posed as dead off-worlders, the chances were we could get off the planet without raising the suspicions of the Fertillan Guard. All that was needed was a couple of coffins and some fake documents, and they were easy to procure.

But I didn't like it.

Travelling in a catatonic state inside a casket meant handing control of my body over to someone else. It wasn't even someone I trusted – it was Patti.

So when I looked into Terri's cryo-pod, the fear of being trapped inside something very similar made me tremble.

"No," I said.

"Why not?" said Keya.

She genuinely seemed not to understand. Even Stephen, who was going to have to 'die' with me, seemed to accept it.

"I'll give you five reasons why not." I pointed to each of the other cryo-pods in turn. All of them still contained the dried corpses of the people sealed inside of them. "Five dead bodies."

"Rob's looked at all of the pods and only one of them had a genuine malfunction," she said. "The other four succumbed to a power failure and the system decided to divert all available power to one of the pods, keeping Terri alive. She's living proof the technology works."

I looked across at Terri who was watching from the door. She shrunk back into the shadows at the mention of her name. "The technology is centuries old," I pointed out. "It's like asking me to put on a spacesuit from the days of the early pioneers and take a space walk."

"Rob is confident there's little to no risk. He says they made things to last back in those days."

"Rob is a *dentist*," I reminded her. "He's not an expert in cryo-sleep, he's not even a doctor!"

"You won't be going into full cryo-sleep," said Keya. "Just enough to fool the Fertillan Guards if they decide to inspect the body transport boxes. Patti will revive you when you're safely in space."

"It's a good plan," said Stephen.

I shook my head. "No, it isn't. There's too much that can go wrong. Even beyond the fact that we're relying on a dentist, ancient equipment that's already killed five people and an ex-pirate."

I walked away from Terri's cryo-pod and out of the cryo-chamber.

"Cassy!" Stephen called after me. I ignored him.

Minutes later, he found me in the propagation chamber under the pinkish light that mimicked the Fertillan sun and surrounded by the little shoots of green that promised to grow into plants. He put an arm around my shoulders and pulled me close. I thought about shaking him off, but I didn't want to start a conflict.

"I'm scared too," he said.

I breathed in the musty smell of the dirt, the moisture and the sprouting life around us. "Keya says this room is inspirational."

"I suppose it is," said Stephen.

"The plants don't care about any of this," I said. "If they have dirt, enough water, enough light and whatever it is they need from the air, then they're happy. You don't see plants assassinating each other or sending each other to jail."

"Plants don't have all the fun," said Stephen. "They grow rooted to the spot so they can't run away when someone tries to eat them."

I almost laughed. "I never thought of that."

Stephen gave my shoulder another squeeze. "We have to run away, Cassy. And soon."

"I'd rather run – really run – than hide in a coffin. If I'm going to die, I'd rather do it fighting with an EEW in my hand."

"You're not going to die, only pretend to. I think this is the best plan. It gets us out of here, off the planet and away from Fertillan space."

81

"If nothing goes wrong," I pointed out.

"You have no faith in people."

"And you have too much."

"Nevertheless, I'm going to do it."

I thought about it for a moment. All I could think of were the desiccated remains of the woman lying in the first pod we inspected, except in my imagination, the dead woman wore my face. "I don't know…"

"You don't have to decide just yet. Rob is going to get the cryo equipment ready to put in the body transport boxes. But once he's ready, I'm going to leave and I'd like you to come with me."

CHAPTER ELEVEN

FOUND TERRI IN the cryo-chamber next to the pod where her
father had died. She had removed the lid so she could see the
whole of his wizened body. I tried not to look at his desiccated,
wrinkled face or think of what might happen to me if our plan to
escape went wrong.

I approached her slowly, with deliberate footsteps which
sounded on the floor so as not to alarm her. There were tears in
her eyes when she looked up. She said nothing for a moment as
she stared at my hair, my eyes and the clothes I was wearing. "You
look different," she said.

I ran my fingers through what was left of my hair. Keya had cut
it strikingly short for me and run it through with streaks of grey to
make me look older. I was wearing contact lenses that turned the
irises of my eyes green and an off-worlder costume with a closely
fitted jacket and long skirt which was uncomfortable, but made

me look more like a wealthy woman from one of the commerce colonies. "Different is the idea," I said. "If anyone checks inside the coffins, they will see exactly what they expect to see from the documentation: two dead off-worlders."

"I want to go into space with you," said Terri.

"We've already discussed this, it's too dangerous," I said. "Even if we could find another coffin and the cryo equipment to take you with us, the strain on your body of going back into cryo-sleep so soon after you've woken up could be too much."

"But I want to find Eden. It's the only place where people I knew might have survived."

"It's been at least two, maybe three generations since they left, Terri. If Eden exists and is still out there, they will all be dead by now. You understand that, don't you?"

"It's so difficult because it seems like only weeks ago to me." She wiped her tears on her sleeve. "It's hard to imagine that they will have had children and their children will have had children. It's those people I might be able to meet."

"You will find another way into space," I said. "But we're about ready to leave. If you want to say goodbye to Stephen, this is your last chance."

She shook her head and reached down into the pod where her father lay. "Dad kept the location of Eden with him in case it was lost while we were asleep."

She took the hand of the dead man – a spindly collection of bones covered in wrinkled skin and clasped into a fist – and tried to prise open his fingers. But, after generations of being kept in the same position, they had fused tight. I turned away as she forced them open and heard the grotesque snap of ancient bones breaking into pieces. It was followed by a quiet thump and, as I turned back, I saw the silver sphere of a memory ball roll under what was left of her father's leg. Terri reached under his body to retrieve it and offered it to me.

"I want you to have it," she said, letting it sit in the palm of her outstretched hand. "You can find Eden and, when you do, you can come and get me."

I wrapped my hand around her fingers and curled them back over the ball so it was held in her fist. "You keep it," I said. "When you go into space, you can find Eden yourself."

Stephen ran into the cryo-chamber. "Cassy, we have to go now!"

Even through the brown of his contact lenses, I saw the urgency in his face. He, like me, was disguised as an off-worlder with his hair dyed a yellowish blonde and wearing a closely cut light grey suit with collarless shirt.

"What's going on?" I said.

"The Fertillan Guard are here."

"What?!"

He looked behind me at Terri. "Get upstairs and stay with Keya; pretend you're one of the staff." He grabbed my hand. "Cassy, come on!"

He pulled me out into the lab and towards the stairs.

I let go of his hand to hitch up my skirt and follow him up the stairs. "How did they find us? Did someone tip them off? Did they follow Freddi's daughter?"

"Could just be a lucky patrol," said Stephen, turning back to look at me down the stairs and putting a finger to his lips to tell me to be quiet.

Above us, I heard the sound of someone hammering loudly on the front door and Keya's voice trying to sound calm as she called out: "We're closed! Surgery opens at 9am tomorrow morning."

Emerging from the store cupboard, I looked through the open door to reception to see Keya standing by the locked front door with a face as white as the dentist's tunic she had put on.

"This is the Fertillan Guard!" came a man's voice from outside. "If you don't open this door, I have the authority to break it down."

"Just a minute!" she called out. "I need to get the key."

She ushered me to run up the stairs to the surgeries and I dashed after Stephen, knowing that she couldn't stall the Fertillan Guard for long. We headed down the corridor above to Surgery Five and entered.

Doctor Robbi Harrist looked up from an equipment tray at the back of the surgery as he thrust two full syringes and some surgical wipes into the pocket of his dentist's tunic. He swivelled to where two body boxes were sitting on the side with their lids open ready to receive their corpses. He snapped the lid of the nearest one shut and picked up one end.

"Stephen, help me with this, can you?"

"What are you doing?" I said.

"I can't put you into cryo-sleep up here," said Rob. "The guards will find you. If they suspect you've been hiding out here, your disguise won't be enough to fool them."

"Then where are you taking the box?"

"There's a van waiting out the back."

"There's a back way out of this place?" Almost nowhere on Fertilla had a back entrance. At least, not the houses or smaller buildings.

"They put it in when the place was a hospital during the plague. When people came for help, they didn't like to see the dead bodies going out the front door. The Fertillan Guard won't know it's there, but only if we go *now!*"

Stephen reached into his pocket for the EEW he had taken from the guard outside the jail and pressed it into my hand. "Take this," he said and grabbed the other end of the body box to help Rob carry it.

I went out first and stood ready with the EEW facing towards the stairs while the men carried the box to the other end of the corridor. I glanced behind me briefly to see them disappear through a door which I hadn't even seen was there until they opened it.

The sound of banging from downstairs became louder and I knew it wasn't long before the guards made good on their promise to break it down. Back in the surgery, the other box was waiting for me with its padded lining that disguised the cryo-sleep equipment underneath. I couldn't leave without it and I knew it would be too heavy for me to lift on my own, so I prayed for the men to hurry back before I ended up in a shoot-out with the Deity knows how many Fertillan Guards.

Stephen and Rob emerged back through the hidden door and ran into the surgery as the final bang from downstairs turned into a crash. The sound of booted feet landing on the waiting room floor was accompanied by a rain of falling debris. I heard Keya start to protest that she had been about to unlock the door, but someone barking orders drowned her out. "Fan out! Search everywhere!"

"Drakh! Come on!" I whispered urgently as Stephen and Rob carried out the second box.

They ran – as best they could with such a heavy object – towards the door as I backed up the corridor behind them, with the EEW aimed straight ahead of me and expecting to hear the sound of Fertillan Guard boots marching up the stairs at any moment.

Stephen and Rob went through the hidden door and I followed to find myself standing on a narrow metal platform on the rear of the building that led down some steep, narrow steps to ground level. The light was subdued, as it was evening in Londos, but the vista of a row of houses belonging to another street was clear on the other side of the quiet road beneath.

Parked close to the bottom of the stairs was a van with the words 'Undertaker' written on the side and its back doors open waiting for us.

I shut the door I had just stepped through and clattered down the metal stairs after Stephen and Rob.

At the bottom, I hopped into the back of the van to find there was barely enough room for the three of us in between the two body boxes. Rob lifted both lids and, as I looked at the padding inside, they appeared even more to look like our coffins.

"Stephen, you first," said Rob as he pulled one of the syringes from his pocket.

Stephen glanced across at me and I saw, for the first time, the fear in his eyes over what we were about to do. He almost climbed into the box, but at the last minute, seemed to change his mind and stepped over it to get to me. He wrapped his arms around me and I felt the comforting warmth of his body. I savoured the moment, but knew it had to be fleeting.

"We haven't got much time," said Rob.

Stephen relinquished the embrace. "Good luck, Cassy."

He turned away and clambered into the box behind him.

"Good luck, Stephen," I whispered.

He lay down and gave me a final look with his disguised brown eyes before he closed them to prepare himself to be sedated ahead of his body being brought to the brink of death. His complexion had already taken on the pallor of a dead person as anxiety had drained the colour from his face.

Pushing up Stephen's sleeve, Rob wiped the skin with a swab and sank the needle of a syringe into his vein. Stephen flinched at the pinprick, the sedative was pushed into his system and his breathing slowed.

Rob placed the lid over the top of Stephen's body, the seals clicked into place and the cryo equipment started to work on taking over his bodily functions and lowering them to a minimal level.

"Now you," he said, looking to me.

I hesitated and clasped the EEW even tighter in my hand.

I looked down into the empty coffin – *my* coffin – and pushed aside my fears so I could bring myself to step inside. The padding was cold and the sides of the box so enclosed that it was difficult to wiggle myself into position and straighten the long skirt which had bunched up around my knees.

"Lie still," said Rob as he exposed my arm and sterilised the skin above one of my veins.

"Promise me I'm not going to die in here," I said.

"I promise," he said.

The needle entered my skin, I felt the cool of the liquid from the syringe mingle with the warmth of my blood, the thoughts of the guards finding the hidden door, the metal steps and the van faded into nothing and the blackness of sleep took me.

CHAPTER TWELVE

I DREW IN A massive breath like my lungs had found air after starving in the vacuum of space. Instinctively, I moved to sit up, but a hand pushed me back down.

"Take it slowly." It was a woman's voice.

My eyes tried to focus, but they were blurry and my eyelids scraped across the lenses covering my irises.

"You're safe," said the voice. "Take your time. Breathe slow and steady."

I willed myself to obey. I felt the solid beat of my heart as it took newly-enriched oxygenated blood around my system and restored life to my body. Blinking free my contact lenses, I allowed my eyes to adjust to the light.

Looking over me was someone with bright blonde hair. I remembered how Stephen had coloured his hair as part of his disguise and, I thought for a moment, it might be him. But, as my brain made sense of the images I was seeing, the features of the face coalesced into Patti.

"I'm safe?" My throat was dry and my tongue almost stuck to my mouth as it formed the words.

"Of course you are," said Patti. "It was my plan. It was a good plan."

I put my hands out and felt the sides of the body box that contained me. I slid my palms up to the top, rested on the edge and pulled myself up to sitting.

"Steady," said Patti as she leant over to help.

I was going to push her away, but a sudden feeling of nausea came over me and I ended up allowing her to take some of my weight.

My stomach spasmed and I retched over the side of the box. Patti jumped back as I was sick so violently, my half-digested food leapt directly from my throat to the floor. Some of it must have splashed up and hit her because I heard her groan.

I panted over the side of the box, looking down at the pool of vomit on the floor and spat the last of it from my mouth. My stomach felt unsettled, but I didn't think it was going to spasm again.

Patti brought me a towel and a mug of water. "By the Deity, Cassy! Don't you know you're supposed to have an empty stomach before you go into cryo-sleep?"

"Sorry." My throat rasped. I took a sip of the water. It was cool and enlivening. "We had to leave in a hurry."

"You could have vomited in the box and choked to death!"

"I was more worried about being shot or captured."

"Hmm," was Patti's only response. "I suppose, if you're arguing with me, you must be all right."

I wiped my mouth with the towel and took on more water. I had the most horrendous headache, but I was able to sit up properly and take a look at my surroundings.

I was in the cargo hold of Patti's ship. Although one cargo hold looks very much like another, I had spent a long time there the first time Patti had smuggled me off a planet and there was something about the confined space stacked with crates that was horribly familiar.

"Where's Stephen?" I said.

Patti pointed over to a second body box towards the back of the hold. "I wanted to wake him up first, but the boxes weren't labelled and I had to take pot luck. Unfortunately, I got you."

I pushed at the sides of my box again, but I was still woozy. "Get me out of this thing, will you?"

Patti gave me a hand and I climbed out.

I made it to Stephen's casket. The lid was off and he was lying still and serene inside. His eyes were closed, which made me wonder why we had bothered with the contact lenses in the first place, and his yellowish blonde hair made the pale skin of his sleeping face seem paler.

"I started the revival process about ten minutes after you," said Patti. "So it won't be long now."

Stephen's chest rose and fell with a shallow breath. I reached in and touched his hand. It was cooler than mine, but not icy cold like a lifeless body. I felt his wrist for a pulse and detected a single beat under my fingertips.

"Where are we?" I said to Patti.

"The cargo hold."

"I meant, where are we in space?"

"Less than a day's journey from Serilla. I thought it was best to get away from the Fertillan system, so I made the short jump."

"Serilla has strong ties to Fertilla," I said. It was where I had first met Stephen. He was commanding a ship of Fertillan Guards who swooped in and arrested me while the local authorities turned a blind eye. A strange memory of a first encounter with a man I became so close to.

"I wouldn't worry. This is a temporary holding position while you figure out your next move. It's all part of the plan. I told you, Cassy, I make good plans."

Stephen breathed again. He looked less pale.

After a few more minutes, he drew in an enormous breath and his eyes flickered.

"Stephen? Stephen, it's Cassy."

His breathing became regular. His pulse under my fingers beat stronger. His eyes opened and focussed on me. "Cassy?" His voice was dry and croaky.

"Yes, I'm here."

"I'm not dead?"

I laughed. "No, you're not dead."

"That's good."

Patti fetched him a mug of water and both of us helped him to sit up.

Stephen took on water with short, quick sips. "Thank you for doing this for us, Patti," he said.

"I didn't do it for you, I did it for Freddi," she said.

A device strapped to her wrist bleeped. "That's the ship calling me. I have to go."

I watched her leave through the door to the cargo hold and made sure she didn't lock it behind her. She did not. Unlike the previous time I had travelled in her ship. Perhaps she really had changed.

I turned back to see Stephen was trying to get out of the box on his own.

"Whoa! Let me help you."

I took one of his hands as the other rested on the side. He swung out one leg in the most ungainly manner and brought the other one down to follow it. As the second foot joined the first, he lost his balance and toppled onto me.

"Sorry, I'm a bit dizzy," he said.

I grabbed hold of him as he regained his balance and we found ourselves close, in each other's arms, with me looking up in his face now flushed with colour, but still with the strange brown eyes and framed in a halo of yellowish blonde hair.

"It's good to be alive, Cassy," he said.

"Yes."

He reached down to kiss me and I anticipated the warmth of his lips touching mine. But his face suddenly squinted into a revolted expression, the colour drained from his cheeks and he turned away from me.

He leant over while his stomach spasmed, the effects of cryo-sleep caught up with him and he was sick all over the floor of Patti's cargo hold.

I FOUND PATTI in her control room. It was a compact space with three consoles jammed into a triangular area at the front of her ship. Quite small compared to the control room on my ship, but quite normal for a freight vessel of that size.

Stephen had followed me up there. He had stopped being ill and the only after-effects seemed to be his own embarrassment at throwing up in front of me and a headache, which he said was thumping through his brain like it was trying to attract his attention. I knew how he felt: I had exactly the same headache.

"Is everything okay?" I asked Patti.

"Everything is going to plan," she said.

A voice came over the communicator. "Patti, are you there?"

Hearing a familiar voice was such a surprise that I thought I might have misheard. I looked to Patti for confirmation. "Is that Freddi?"

She nodded and hit the green reply pad on the screen in front of her. "Yes, I'm here. I've got someone who wants to talk to you."

"Freddi?" I leant forward into the microphone embedded into the console. "Freddi, is that you?"

"Cassy?"

By the way he said my name, there was no doubt it was him, and a rush of emotion caused moisture to well in my eyes. It was silly of me. I decided my reaction had to be the residual effects of cryo-sleep.

"Yes, Freddi, it's me! How are you? How did you find us?"

"It was Patti's idea. She suggested meeting here."

"What happened? I was told you'd been arrested."

"They eventually let me go," said Freddi. "There was no evidence I was ever involved and so they finally had to admit they couldn't hold me any longer. I allowed them to carry out a thorough search of the ship to make sure I hadn't stowed you away somewhere, then they let me leave the Fertillan system. I think they were glad to get rid of me."

Stephen came forward to join us at the communications console. "Does that mean he's brought your ship?"

The question was directed at me, but it was Patti who answered. "Yes. Which, in turn, means I can get rid of you two and be on my way. Freddi will need to send over a shuttle to collect you, this vessel is only equipped with an escape pod."

"Thanks, Patti," I said.

She smiled. "I think I mentioned to you before that I come up with good plans."

CHAPTER THIRTEEN

THE AIRLOCK DOOR opened in the cargo hold of Patti's ship and revealed the snaking, white tunnel that linked her vessel to Freddi's shuttle. The air seemed to sigh as the pressurised atmosphere within the tube of connecting fabric mingled with the environment where Stephen and I were standing.

A grey, space-suited figure floated towards us. Head first, like a slow-motion torpedo flying in the weightlessness of space. It was reassuring to see Freddi's two green eyes through the visor of his helmet as he tugged at the guide rope along the inside of the tunnel and propelled himself faster towards us.

He reached out his gloved hand into Patti's ship and I grabbed it to help him as he used me as leverage to pull his feet forward and allowed them to find the solid floor where he could stand in the artificial gravity. Tucked under his arm he carried two spare spacesuits. They were the minimal protection, easily manoeuvrable ones, not the bulky armoured ones used for carrying out maintenance or long space walks. He unclipped the line around his waist from the guide rope in the tunnel and took off his helmet.

Freddi shook out the strands of his ginger and grey hair and I saw they had grown a little since his pre-wedding haircut and had resumed their more familiar shaggy look. He smiled at me and it felt good to be back with my best friend.

Even though he was wearing the spacesuit and it was cumbersome, I put my arms around him and gave him a hug. "I'm so glad you're all right."

Despite the stiff material of his spacesuit, I could still feel him resist my display of emotion. "I'm glad too, Cassy," he said.

"Cassy doesn't greet *me* like that," remarked Stephen, who had been standing quietly and patiently beside me.

"Perhaps that's because you decided to marry someone else," said Freddi.

Stephen's smile became fixed on his face. "Yes, well," he faltered. "That plan didn't turn out so good, as it happens."

When I released Freddi, I stood back and examined his face more closely. There were no fresh scars, his skin looked a healthy colour and he appeared well nourished. "Are you sure you're okay? The Fertillan Guard didn't hurt you?"

He shrugged it off. "They locked me up and they questioned me – endlessly – but there was no torture. I think they already knew that I couldn't tell them anything useful." He paused and looked me over. "What have you done to your hair?"

I ran my hand through the short, straggly strands and hated how it felt. "Oh, it was part of my disguise. Do you like it?"

"It suits you longer," he said, with typical Freddi honesty.

The internal door to the cargo hold opened and Patti appeared.

She did not come in, but stood in the doorway, leaning against the frame with her arms folded in order to watch us from a distance. I had only glanced over at the noise, but she held Freddi's attention somehow and the two of them stared at each other silently across the room.

Freddi broke eye contact and pulled out the two spacesuits he was carrying and handed one each to me and Stephen. "You might want these."

We took them from him and he walked over to see Patti. The two of them soon started up a conversation in whispered tones that I couldn't make out.

I stepped into the legs of the spacesuit and tried to push my skirt inside. It was a pointless exercise and I ended up taking the wretched thing off.

Stephen, in trousers, found it much easier to step into his suit. "I thought we didn't need these for walking onto another ship across a connecting tunnel," he said. "It's fully pressurised with breathable air and heat."

"Strictly, we don't," I said, as I manoeuvred my arms into the sleeves. "But once you've seen a tunnel set adrift by a piece of colliding space debris, you're never going to want to step into one unprotected ever again. Tumbling into the vacuum to freeze to death while you gasp for non-existent air is a horrible way to die."

Stephen paled at the thought as he secured the final seals of his suit.

A delicate female laugh sang out from the doorway. Patti's laugh was so different to her people-smuggling ex-pirate image that it was difficult to believe the noise came from her. But I glanced over in her direction to see she had thrown her head back with a smile that was so wide it showed off her teeth to be almost as white as her bright blonde hair. Whatever the joke was, Freddi was clearly enjoying it too.

"What's going on with those two?" Stephen whispered.

"It's best not to ask," I said.

I helped Stephen put his helmet on and then called over to Freddi before Stephen gave me a hand with mine.

Freddi said something to Patti that, again, I didn't hear and took a few steps backwards. He gave her a little wave, she smiled in reply and went back to folding her arms.

We carried out the final checks on our spacesuits, clipped the safety lines to the rope and climbed into the white of the tunnel for the weightless swim to the shuttle.

I BREATHED IN the air of my own spaceship and sensed the glorious smell of home.

It was such an elusive smell that it defied description. Not like other people's ships, which always seemed to have a hint of the grease that kept the machines lubricated, the lingering odour of the meal they had most recently consumed or the detergent they used for washing. My home may have had all of those things, but they were undetectable to me because they were normal. My nostrils sensed the familiar and my brain filtered them out. It coddled me in its feeling of safety and I was able to truly relax for the first time since I had left to go to Stephen's wedding.

Freddi suggested setting a course in normal space for Serilla.

We were close, he argued, and that meant we didn't have to expend any expensive qubition to use the Quantum Entanglement Drive to open a wormhole. But I wasn't ready to go anywhere without a solid plan and I wanted to sit down and discuss our next move in the crew lounge first.

The crew lounge was also where Freddi kept his beer in a not-so-secret stash at the back of a cupboard in the kitchenette area and I was keen to take advantage.

"I hope you've managed to stock up on beer again since we last drank it all?" I said as we walked down the corridor.

Freddi glanced back at Stephen. "She's been back barely five minutes and already she's stealing my beer!"

"Captain's prerogative," I told him.

He rolled his eyes, but I knew he didn't really care. It was just so good to be back together again on the ship.

Freddi paused when we reached the door to the crew lounge. "Oh," he said. "I forgot to mention that we picked up a couple of passengers."

"Passengers?" I said.

But he had walked inside before I managed to get an answer out of him.

I followed and immediately heard a woman's voice call my name.

"Cassy!" Terri leapt up off the couch and came rushing over. "And Stephen – you're here!"

She seemed as excited as a child. Her face had much more colour than I remembered it having in the underground lab and her body had started to fill out a bit, although the shirt and slacks she wore still hung off her limbs as if they belonged to someone else.

"Terri!" I said with surprise. "What are you doing here?"

Keya emerged from the kitchenette clasping a steaming mug with her fingers wrapped around it to warm them. "Terri wanted to go into space," she explained.

"Keya," I said. "Freddi didn't mention you were here."

"You don't mind, do you?" She took a sip of her drink.

"Of course I don't mind." I threw a glance across to Freddi. "It would have been nice to have been told, that's all."

"Sorry," he said. "It's been a bit of a week."

Stephen clapped his hands together behind me and the sudden noise made me jump. "Did someone mention something about beer?" he said.

Freddi nodded. "I'll get it." He went into the kitchenette while Stephen took up position on the couch, leaving Terri to choose one of our modest and ageing chairs to sit in. It seemed to overwhelm her skinny body with its wide, padded arms.

I pulled Keya aside. She looked tired. She was dressed smartly in matching sandy brown tunic and trousers and her make-up was neatly applied, but there was fatigue beneath the rouge of her cheeks and the maroon of her lipstick.

"What happened after I left? Are you all right? Is Rob all right?"

"The Fertillan Guard were looking for you and they didn't find you, so he was able to claim you were never there."

"What about *you*?"

She shrugged. "My lab was trashed again. At least this time, being on a planet, it was a bit difficult to blow the whole thing up. Rob told them he rented out the basement to a group of scientists and claimed not to know they were carrying out illegal food research there. Terri and I maintained our cover as part of the dental staff which, thankfully, they didn't check. After that, I couldn't stay."

"I'm sorry I got you into this, Keya."

"I got myself into this," she said. "I could have taken a teaching job somewhere, but my heart has always been in research. I wanted to do something to change the galaxy for the better. I just wish the galaxy didn't keep fighting against me."

Freddi brought over a beer for me and I took it over to the couch where I sat next to Stephen, while Keya took her hot drink – which I surmised was some sort of weak tea – over to another one of the chairs.

I brought the bottle to my lips. The beer was both sweet and sharp, which revived and relaxed me at the same time. I allowed my body to sink into the padded material of the couch while, next to me, Stephen accepted the beer Freddi handed to him.

It reminded me of the first time Stephen and I had sat there together and talked – really talked. Up until that point, aside from an occasional glimpse, I hadn't really seen him as a man. He had been Prince Stephen Regellan, the member of the royal family that I had learnt about at school and seen in the news broadcasts. He had been Marshal Commander Regellan, the head of the Fertillan Guard and someone to avoid running into if at all possible. But, when he had come aboard my ship, and we had sat on that very couch drinking the last of Freddi's secret stash of beer, we found ourselves laughing together and talking as if we had known each other for years. It was the start of me falling in love with him. The memory seemed such a long time ago. After all that had happened since then, my feelings for him remained, but circumstances meant I could not allow them to flourish, no matter how much I would like them to.

Freddi, holding his beer like he didn't quite know what to do with it, ambled around in the middle of the seating area without anywhere to sit. I was about to shuffle up on the sofa to make room for him to sit next to me, when Terri leapt up from her chair.

"Why don't you sit here?" she said. "I have something to show Cassy."

She reached into her trouser pocket and pulled out the memory ball which she had prised from her dead father's fingers.

"Don't bother Cassy with that now," said Freddi, relaxing back into the chair. "She's barely got back."

"No, it's okay," I said. I was intrigued to see what exactly had been so important that a man felt the need to take it with him into cryo-sleep.

Terri took the memory ball over to the screen embedded in the wall in front of us. The light glinted off its silver, spherical surface as she pushed it into the receptor beneath the screen and it was drawn into the mechanism. Terri fumbled her way around the touch controls until something appeared and she stepped away so we could see.

A starscape filled the screen with, at one edge, the round dot of a location marker.

"Where's that?" asked Stephen.

"It's Eden," said Terri with wide-eyed enthusiasm. "Or, where Eden should be."

Freddi sipped his beer. "I keep telling her we can't go there."

"Why not?" Terri demanded.

"Partly because we have no money and need to take an actual paying job before we run out of food and fuel," said Freddi. "But mostly because it's on the other side of the Rim."

"Not much of a problem," said Stephen. "You'll need more qubition to wormhole to the other side of the galaxy, that's all."

"No, I meant the *other side* of the Rim," said Freddi. "As in, the *outside* of the Rim, *beyond* the rim, *external* to the galaxy itself."

"That's impossible," I said.

I handed my beer to Stephen and went over to the screen to get a closer look. The map was clear. It showed a small segment of the Obsidian Rim with its sparsely dispersed collection of stars at the habitable edge of the galaxy. Now I was close I could see the faint band of grey, which represented the scrambled magnetic barrier surrounding the Rim. The marker was on the other side of it. Travel to that point in space might have been possible before the Oblivion War, but not after the qubition bombs exploded. They had reacted with the gaseous halo on the galaxy's edge and caused humanity to be trapped in a prison of its own making.

"Freddi says it *is* possible," said Terri. "He said you travelled through the barrier before."

"I said no such thing! I said we *encountered* the barrier before."

"As I recall, we crashed into it," I said. "We had to pay for repairs."

"Which is what I told her," insisted Freddi. "I told her, we pierced the barrier which suggests it might be possible to travel through it in normal space, even if wormhole travel is impossible. But I didn't say we could go. I said she would need to find someone willing to take her after we drop her and Keya off wherever they want to be dropped off."

I peered again at the map. "Are you sure this thing is accurate? Even if you could travel beyond the Rim, why would you want to? There's nothing there except a two million light year gap between us and the Andromeda Galaxy."

"Because it's a good place to hide," said Terri. "Away from people who would rather have the project destroyed, away from chance discovery, away from pirates."

The ship jolted. I was knocked sideways and took a couple of steps before I regained my balance.

Freddi was on his feet. "What was that?"

I looked to the ceiling. "Ellen?"

The mature, female voice of the ship's computer answered. "An approaching ship fired at us. I apologise for not alerting you to its presence sooner, Cassy, but it was on course to uninhabited space where I assumed it was preparing for wormhole travel."

As she spoke, I swiped the Eden map from the screen and brought up the live sensor readings. It clearly showed an approaching ship. "Have you got a visual?"

"Yes, Cassy," said Ellen.

The screen went dark as it showed the view of space from the ship. In the top corner was the bright Serillan star which generated enough light to show the blocky outline of a ship painted in the brown colour of the Fertillan Guard.

"Drakh!" I said.

Stephen got up. "What is it?"

"They've found us."

CHAPTER FOURTEEN

I RAN INTO THE control room.

Freddi was already at his console. "They're targeting our QED so we can't wormhole out. I'm turning the ship so it's facing away from them, but they can manoeuvre just as fast as we can."

The ship shuddered again. I staggered forward and grabbed hold of the base of my central command console which had two screens rising up from it. I brought up the data of the ship's systems on the left display. "Ellen? What's the damage?"

"Minimal, Cassy," she replied from the speakers above. "The shielding in that area is holding. For now."

Stephen, Keya and Terri appeared at the doorway. "What can we do?" said Stephen.

"You better sit down, this could get bumpy," I said.

"But keep out of the way!" Freddi yelled.

The three of them slunk in and found seats at the three crew positions that Freddi and I rarely used. The control room was a generous space, as it was built for a crew of five, but Freddi and I found we did just fine with the two of us.

My console bleeped urgently. A call was coming through from the other ship. "Ellen, can you patch external communications through to Freddi's position? I'd rather the Fertillan Guard don't see that I'm here."

"Of course, Cassy," she said. "They're requesting visual as well as audio."

"Fine," said Freddi.

The background hum of another ship's systems came over the speakers, indicating the link was live.

"What the vac are you doing?" Freddi bellowed at the camera on his console. "You attacked us with no warning, no justification."

A man's voice replied. It was young, but confident. "This is Commander Jensen Everade of the Fertillan Guard. Cease manoeuvres and prepare to be boarded."

"On what grounds?" demanded Freddi.

I adjusted the controls on my console so the visual feed from the Fertillan Guard ship appeared on my right screen while my camera remained turned off. The image of the man suited his voice. He was clean-shaven with a chin almost as smooth as a boy's, while his short, military-style haircut revealed he was starting to lose his hair early. He was in uniform, but had dispensed with his Fertillan Guard hat so he was able to stare at the camera with unshaded deep brown eyes.

"I have reason to believe you are harbouring fugitives. Namely, the former Prince, Stephen Regellan, and Individual Sesaan Cassandra."

"You searched this ship inside and out before I left Fertilla," said Freddi. "You know that's a lie."

"Cease manoeuvres and prepare to be boarded," ordered Everade.

Stephen got up from his seat and stood at the opposite side of Freddi's screens so Freddi could see him and Everade could not. Stephen swiped his hand in front of his throat in a cutting motion.

A flick of Freddi's eyes was enough to indicate he had seen and understood.

"Message received, Commander," Freddi told Everade in a matter-of-fact way. "Stand by."

He flicked a control and the background hum of the other ship cut off as communication was severed.

"Let me speak to Everade," said Stephen.

"No, it'll confirm you're on board," said Freddi.

"They know that already, or have a strong suspicion. It won't make any difference. I know the man: he's one of my brightest and most ambitious commanders."

"It's worth a shot," I said.

"You can try if you like," said Freddi. "But I don't think it'll do any good."

I looked up to the speakers in the ceiling. "Ellen, can you patch the feed through to Console Four?"

"Of course, Cassy."

Stephen went back to his screen and, after a moment familiarising himself with the controls, opened the link to the Fertillan Guard ship.

Everade's expression changed immediately as he saw Stephen's face and seemed to almost stand to attention at the sight of his former commanding officer. "Sire!"

"Hello, Jensen," said Stephen in a warm and friendly tone. "How are you?"

"Pleased to see you, Sire. But I'm afraid I've been ordered to bring you in."

"I understand," said Stephen. "I'm surprised to see you out here, Everade. One of my last duties was to grant you leave. It was your son's birthday, wasn't it?"

"Yes, Sire." Everade shifted uncomfortably at the disclosure of his personal information. "All leave was cancelled following the escape of the Queen's assassin."

"I'm sorry to hear you weren't able to be with your son on his birthday, Jensen, I really am."

"I still have orders to bring you in, Sire. Turn your airlock towards us and open it ready for boarding."

"Of course. I shall get my crew to oblige." Stephen waved an instruction over to Freddi, who must have been visible to Everade over the link.

Freddi looked offended at being ordered about and glanced over to me. I nodded that he should go ahead, but I mouthed an extra instruction of my own: slowly.

Freddi attended to his console and I felt the gentle power of the normal space engines start to turn us.

"Tell me, Jensen," said Stephen to the camera. "How did you find us?"

Everade smiled like he was proud of his achievements. "We put a tracker on Individual Cassandra's ship when we searched it, Sire."

I felt foolish. Caught by a simple tracking device. I glared across at Freddi. He didn't look up from his console, but a flush of embarrassment reddened his cheeks.

"Clever," acknowledged Stephen. "But you can't track a ship through a wormhole."

"No, Sire," agreed Everade. "But we knew the chances were the ship would appear in normal space sooner or later. We deployed as many ships as we could in the most likely systems and then it was only a matter of waiting to detect the signal from the tracker."

Stephen nodded. "And your ship was the one that got lucky."

"Yes, Sire." Everade looked down for a moment, as if checking something on his console, then back up at the camera. "If you don't mind me saying, Sire, you are being unexpectedly compliant."

"What would you do if I resisted?" asked Stephen.

"Blast a hole in your hull, board by force and take you into custody. Alive if possible. Dead if not."

"That's what I thought," said Stephen.

He found the control to cut communications and the speakers fell silent.

Stephen turned to me and Freddi. "He knows I'm bluffing and he knows I won't come quietly."

"Then we wormhole to safety," I said. "Somewhere without any Fertillan Guard ships, where we can find and destroy the tracker."

"They'll sense you firing up the QED before the wormhole's even opened," said Stephen.

"Well, I'm not sitting here and waiting to be captured." I glanced across at Freddi. "Can you shorten the QED sequence? Maybe we can distract them long enough for us to get away."

"No," he said. "QED preparation sequences take the time they take for a reason. One bad calculation and we're wormholing into the middle of a sun or on a collision course with a planet."

Terri, who had been sitting watching and listening to the whole thing, suddenly spoke. "Not if you emerge close to the outer reaches of the Rim." She left her seat and came over. "You can't physically wormhole beyond the Rim, right? So you don't have to be accurate. Just aim and fire."

"Terri," said Keya, coming up to join her. "You can't use this as an excuse to go looking for Eden."

"But you wanted coordinates for a safe place. The hideout for Eden was properly researched before the crew left. That's why my father put the location on the memory ball and took it into cryo-sleep with him. He knew it would be almost impossible to find without that information."

Freddi looked up from his console with a worried expression. "I'm going to need a decision soon. The Fertillan Guard ship has released its shuttle and it's almost lined up with the airlock to access the bay. If we don't let them in soon, they'll blast their way in."

I took a moment to breathe in the air of my own ship which, not so long ago, had felt like the safest place in the galaxy. Now I felt the claws of danger dragging me back to their dark and dank lair. "Then we better let them in."

Freddi saw that I was serious and nodded. "Aye aye, Captain."

"But get those coordinates for Eden off that memory ball and set a course if you can," I told him. "Work with Ellen on whatever data we have from when we crashed into the Rim before and make sure we don't do it again."

Freddi called after me as I headed for the door. "Cassy, we haven't got time for all that."

"You don't have to be accurate. Just aim and fire."

CHAPTER FIFTEEN

STEPHEN AND I stood, unarmed, in the shuttle bay. Ahead of us was the Fertillan Guard shuttle, nestled in alongside my own ship's shuttle which I had bought second hand after the original was taken by pirates. The difference between the two craft was like the difference in status between a prince and a freelance spaceship captain. The oval-shaped Fertillan Guard vessel was pristine without even a scratch from any encounter with space debris and minimal carbon deposits from entering a planet's atmosphere. My shuttle, by contrast, was marked, battered and dented. It had also never attempted to disguise the base metal used to construct it, while its neighbour was painted the same ugly brown as the Fertillan Guard uniforms with a code number on the side, FG:AG1, stencilled in block white lettering.

A crack appeared around the last three digits of the lettering and, with the smoothness of a well-oiled machine, revealed itself to be the ellipse of an opening door. The door was hinged at the bottom and lowered itself down like the slowly dropping jaw of a yawning animal while an embarkation ramp descended from inside.

Stephen turned to me. "I still don't like this plan," he said.

"This is going to work, trust me. I've been bumming around space for a long time and I haven't been killed yet."

"There's always a first time."

I frowned and raised my hands in surrender, ready to be greeted by the Fertillan Guard. Stephen looked doubtful, but followed my lead.

The first Fertillan guardsman or woman emerged from the shuttle and descended down the ramp with a deadly EE rifle ready to shoot the moment either one of us made a false move. He – or she, it was difficult to tell – wore an armoured minimal protection spacesuit in the same brown as the regular uniform with a helmet that had a closed tinted blast shield which hid his or her eyes. It was impressive clothing, but also a compromise between manoeuvrability, protection from the vacuum if they were exposed to space, and shielding from EE blasts.

Stephen had estimated that there would be five armed guards coming across in the shuttle. Overkill, perhaps, but with valuable prisoners, they wouldn't have wanted to take any chances. It was both reassuring and unnerving that he was right, as I counted four more guards descend down the ramp in armoured suits. They stopped in the bay and took up position with their EE rifles pointing directly at us so I could be assured that, should we make any sudden moves, we could expect to be killed five times over.

The lead guard barked an order at us through a communications speaker in their helmet. "Turn around!" The voice was female, but otherwise devoid of personality.

I exchanged a glance with Stephen and we slowly turned so we had our backs to them.

"Kneel and put your hands behind you."

It was the bit I hated. I had been arrested enough times to know it was the position in which I was the most vulnerable. So I hesitated and it took one of the guards to put a hand on my shoulder and force me down. As my knees hit the hard floor, I remembered Stephen's reluctance to go with my plan and I had to push away my own doubts before they clouded my mind.

My right arm was grabbed from where it hung at my side and pulled behind me. A solid, metal cuff secured my wrist. My other arm was forced to join it and my hands were locked into position behind my back. The guard tightened the cuffs so they cut into my flesh and rubbed against the bone.

My brain screamed a silent order: *Now, now, now!*

A siren blared all around us and I smiled to myself as the plan swung into action.

The outer bay door clanked with age as it began to open and expose us all to the vacuum of space. Air rushed past at the release of pressure: vital, life-giving air that Stephen and I needed to live. Fully aware that it would soon be all gone, I took a gulp into my lungs.

Beneath me, through the floor, I felt the vibration of the Quantum Entanglement Drive surge into life. A feeling only a captain of a ship can understand. A vibration that I hoped, in all the confusion, the guards would not notice.

"What are you doing?" yelled the woman through her helmet, her voice suddenly sounding thin in the dispersing atmosphere.

"It's not me!" I protested. "I can't do anything with my hands cuffed behind my back!"

I don't know if she heard and I don't know if she even cared because, as I turned my head to look at her, I saw she was suddenly distracted by the two guards nearest the shuttle who had panicked and were running back up the ramp. The lead guard gesticulated at her two subordinates who had cuffed us.

I was grabbed and hauled to my feet and I struggled as I was pulled backwards towards the shuttle. In front of me, I saw the other guard do the same to Stephen.

"No!" I screamed. "I'll suffocate before I get to the shuttle!" I tried taking another breath to tell them I needed to get into the safety of the ship, but there was not enough air left for speech.

I saw that the narrow strip of black space revealed by the opening bay door was getting wider. Heat, as well as air was being sucked out. I exhaled what little breath I had from my lungs in a puff of gas and moisture that instantly froze into ice crystals.

I felt a rising panic. *Where was my vacking rescue?*

At last, the door to the ship's interior released its seals and swung open. A rush of breathable air blew past me and I gasped to capture some of it for my starving lungs. In the same moment, a streak from an EEW exploded from the corridor into the shuttle bay. The random, unaimed blast, shot between the guards and struck their shuttle without causing any damage. But the distraction was enough for Stephen to break free of his captor and dive for the door. With his hands secured behind him, he fell forward and crashed onto the floor, but he succeeded in making it across the threshold. I tried to yank myself free from the guard who held me by the arm, but his grip was tight and I was weakening. I didn't have long before I passed out.

That's when I saw Freddi. Just a glimpse of his eyes snatching a look around the doorframe before he aimed his EEW. A shot sailed perilously close to my face and struck the guard in the shoulder. The force of the blast knocked him backwards and he let go of my arm.

A pair of women's hands reached out through the doorway as Freddi fired again. I was grabbed around the waist and dragged to safety.

The door must have shut, sealed and locked behind me because I was suddenly aware of being surrounded by warm, still and breathable air. I lay on the floor, gasping down gulps of oxygen-rich breath and shaking from the effects of exposure and fear-induced adrenaline.

I managed to open my eyes and look up into the face of Freddi who was kneeling beside me. I wanted to ask him what was happening, but my body wasn't ready to waste air on speaking.

"Ellen?" Freddi called out to the ship. "What's the status of the Fertillan Guards from the shuttle?"

"They have reboarded. The shuttle bay door is approaching fully open and they are readying to disembark. The main Fertillan Guard ship is re-positioning itself to attack."

The same hands which pulled me to safety were under my back and helping me to sit up. As I rested myself against the wall, I saw that the person helping me was Keya.

"Are you okay, Cassy?" she asked.

I nodded my gratitude. "Who's..." I took a breath. "Flying..." Another breath. "The ship?"

"Terri," said Freddi.

"Terri?!"

"Would you have preferred that she was the one who came down and did the shooting?"

I didn't get a chance to answer because Ellen spoke from above: "Q-burst initiating."

Stephen shuffled to get closer to me and reached out his cuffed hands behind his back. His fingers found mine and held them in an awkward warm and strong grasp. "It was a good plan," he said.

The ship shuddered. It knocked me sideways and I fell onto Stephen's shoulder.

"The Fertillan Guard ship is firing on us," said Ellen. "It's demanding urgent communication."

"It won't risk hitting its own shuttle, surely?" I said.

But I didn't get an answer. A rumble like approaching thunder engulfed the ship and I experienced the familiar, unpleasant feeling of my guts lurching forward as the QED engaged.

CHAPTER SIXTEEN

I RAN TO THE control room with the two halves of my handcuffs flapping at my wrists from where Freddi had severed the middle link with a blast from his EEW.

I came up short as I went through the door when I saw Terri standing at my command console. "We're close to the edge of the Rim," she said. She seemed pleased at her achievement, but also strangely nervous.

I pushed her aside and pulled up the details on both my screens. The presence of the scrambled magnetic barrier was making itself known to the ship's instruments which were sending back fluctuating and nonsensical readings. I brought up the visual feeds from the external cameras and an unwelcome presence loomed large in the image from outside of the shuttle bay. It was the brown oval of the Fertillan Guard shuttle with its white code number, FG:AG1, illuminated by the faint resonance of light emitted from my ship.

"They followed us?" I said.

"I think they got sucked into the wormhole along with us," said Terri.

I glared at her. "You weren't supposed to fire the QED until they were clear!"

"I didn't have any choice. The big ship fired on us. Ellen said if we got hit like that during the q-burst it could have ignited the qubition and blown us up."

"Don't be ridiculous!" I told her. "They wouldn't have risked blowing up their own shuttle and killing their own people."

Stephen had run after me from the shuttle bay and, along with Keya, stood in the doorway recovering his breath and listening to our conversation. "They would," he assured me. "Everade is ambitious. If he thought we were getting away, he wouldn't hesitate to sacrifice some of his crew to stop us."

Freddi, limping from running with his bad hip, pushed Stephen out of the way to get into the control room and headed straight for his console. He looked around at the grim faces of everyone else. "What's happened?"

"We made it to the edge of the Rim, except we seem to have brought the Fertillan Guard with us," I said.

His face hardened as he checked on his screen that what I was telling him was true.

A proximity alarm screeched out from the speakers. I scanned the visual feeds in front of me. My first thought was that the alarm was triggered by the shuttle, but it didn't look to have moved close enough to set it off.

"It's a wormhole!" yelled Freddi.

"What?!"

"A wormhole's opening almost on top of us." Freddi slammed the normal space engines into maximum and the ship lurched forward.

On my screens, I watched as the very fabric of spacetime rippled in front of me. The pinpricks of light from distant stars blinked out of existence like a cloud passing in front of them in the night sky and the undulating black bubbled like boiling water. A hole erupted in the middle, sending out light and energy as it created a pathway in spacetime. The ship shook and the readings on my screen shouted warnings of maximum tolerances.

A dark blob appeared at the centre of the wormhole like the pupil in the iris of a shining eye which expanded as it came towards us.

Freddi changed course and the ship lurched away from the hurtling object which, as it became bigger on my screen, revealed itself to be the blocky brown shape of the Fertillan Guard ship.

"They followed us!" I said.

"I thought you said that was impossible," said Keya, looking back and forth between me and Stephen. "I thought you said they couldn't track us through a wormhole."

"They couldn't using the tracker," said Stephen. "But if they were close enough when we fired up the QED, they might have been able to gather enough data to mimic our destination."

"They're mad!" said Freddi, keeping his attention on the screen in front of him and looking increasingly worried at what it was telling him. "The wormhole's unstable. They fired it up too quickly and too close to ours."

"Everade is ambitious enough to take the chance," said Stephen.

"Then Everade is an idiot," said Freddi.

121

The light and energy spilling from the hole abruptly ceased and the wormhole collapsed. The Fertillan Guard ship came tumbling out – riding on the waves of rippling aftershocks – and on a collision course with its own shuttle.

The shuttle fired its thrusters – but not quick enough to escape – and its parent ship slammed into the rear. The craft rebounded and was sent spinning end over end towards the scrambled magnetic barrier. Its engines fired in a vain attempt to regain control, but the puffs of energy served only to slow it down as it ploughed into the barrier.

Swirls of colour danced around the shuttle's hull in ribbons of vibrant green, electric blue and glowing red as the barrier reacted to its intruder.

The main Fertillan Guard ship had ricocheted from the collision and was sent on a slower, yet equally uncontrolled path, towards the edge of the galaxy. Everade – or his crew – seemed to realise too late what was happening. They fired up their engines, but they had run out of normal space and the energy was released into the fabric of the scrambled magnetic field itself – igniting a display of fireworks in green, blue and red.

It decelerated, but was travelling too fast to stop and its nose plunged into the barrier until it came to a halt: half in and half out of our galaxy.

ON MY RIGHT screen, the Fertillan Guard ship struggled to free itself from the barrier. The more it moved, the more energy sparked around it in eddies of coloured lights. This was not the behaviour of a simple magnetic field – scrambled or not. Other radiation from the electromagnetic spectrum was likely to be present, along with charged particles and possibly gravitational and other forces. Magnetism on its own doesn't create light. Magnetism on its own doesn't fight back when a spacecraft crashes into it.

Not that we could know for sure because the readings we were getting back from the sensors were all over the place. If we were to pass through the barrier to hide out on the other side, we would have to rely on the data we had gathered on our previous encounter and our limited observation of what was happening to the Fertillan Guard ship and its shuttle. The way we had escaped before was to use short engine bursts to move steadily and slowly out of the barrier to avoid aggravating the forces within it. In order to transit right through to the other side, our plan was to fire the engines only as much as necessary in order to glide carefully while causing minimal disruption. It would be like creeping past a sleeping ogre quietly on tiptoes so as not to awake him and incur his wrath. Once beyond the barrier, we would be able to conceal ourselves from our own galaxy just as Eden had done.

In theory. Until we tried it, it was still only a theory.

I rubbed at the marks around my wrists where I had cut off the last of the Fertillan Guard handcuffs and made the final system checks as best I could with the fluctuating readings.

Freddi, at my side at his own console, briefly fired the engines to take us up to the edge of the barrier.

Ellen monitored our power output and our progress in space. "I'm detecting no resistance from the field," she said.

Data continued to bounce around wildly on my left screen. On my right, the feed from an external camera showed the Fertillan Guard ship making progress in extracting itself from the snare.

"Looks like we're leaving just in time," I said.

"Acknowledged," said Freddi. "Entering the outer portion of the barrier now."

The fuzziness of grey and white static broke up the image of the Fertillan Guard ship. The picture stretched and squashed on the screen repeatedly until the whole thing went black.

"Ellen, what happened to the camera feed?" I waited for a reply which didn't come. "Ellen?"

"We've lost the main computer," said Freddi. "Let's hope the controls to the engines are unaffected. I don't fancy going to the engine room and operating them manually."

He fired another short blast for good measure and the ship responded by easing itself forward. Swirls of coloured lights danced at the front of the control room. There was no going back now.

Stephen appeared at the door. He was rubbing the red pressure lines on his wrists where the cuffs had cut into his skin. "Can I help?" he said.

"I thought you were going to wait in the crew lounge with Keya and Terri," I said.

"I've spent my career commanding crews on spaceships. I couldn't just sit there."

"Fine. Take up position at one of the spare consoles. Monitor what you can and be ready to act. But don't do anything without my say-so."

"Yes, Captain," he said without any trace of irony.

But he didn't get as far as the console before a curling ribbon of shining red twisted up from the floor in front of him and arced up and out through the ceiling.

"What was that?" he said, stepping back.

"Charged particles discharging their energy into visible light," said Freddi. "Probably."

"Is it safe?"

Freddi looked doubtfully at the beautiful light display encroaching further into the ship. "Probably."

At that moment, a streak of green leapt from the console Stephen had been heading towards and shot straight at him. Before he had any time to react, it passed straight through his chest and out the other side.

He gasped, jumped sideways and put his hand out to the wall where he rested, breathing quickly.

"Stephen, are you okay?" I asked him.

"I think so," he said, as he stood up straight and tentatively removed his hand.

The lights engulfed us all. They twirled around and through us, drawing patterns in the air with no respect for the boundaries of the ship or our bodies. I watched as a blue one passed straight through my hand and felt nothing. Like the radio waves from the invisible part of the electromagnetic spectrum that pass unseen and undetected through us every day.

"I'm having trouble reaching the engines," said Freddi.

"We can't stop now, we'll be stuck in the barrier," I said.

"I realise that, Cassy. I'm going to try a long, sustained burn. I'm hoping that'll be enough to get us through."

He swiped his hand across the controls. Nothing happened. He did it again. Still no response. I stared at the concentration on his face – I was powerless to do anything else – as he tried a third time. He waited a moment and then he allowed himself a small, satisfied smile. The engines responded and I felt the power surge beneath us.

The coloured lights of the barrier, still twirling and twisting, passed through the control room and out towards the back of the ship until everything around us appeared normal.

Data returned to my left screen. The numbers fluctuated, but nothing like they had done before. The feed from the external camera filled the right screen with the grey and white fuzz of static before the image stabilised into solid black. For a moment I thought the monitor was broken, but then I saw the smudged-looking blob of what had to be another, distant galaxy.

"We're through!" I sighed with relief and leant forward on my console as I let my anxiety flow away.

"Well done!" exclaimed Stephen. He came over to me and swept me up in an exuberant hug. I yelped with surprise, but laughed with my own sense of achievement as he let me go.

Ellen's voice crackled to life over the speakers. "I apologise Cassy, I appear to have been offline," she said.

"Don't worry, Ellen," I said. "We're just glad to have you back."

Stephen went up to Freddi and offered his hand to shake. "Well done, Freddi. Excellent flying."

Freddi ignored Stephen's hand. He didn't even turn to look at him: he was staring at the screen.

"What do you make of that?" he asked, pointing at his console.

A look of concentration came over Stephen's face as he leant over Freddi's shoulder. "Can you zoom in?"

"Yeah," said Freddi. He brushed his hand across the screen.

I was getting frustrated that I couldn't see what the vac was going on. "What is it?"

"Look at camera three," said Freddi.

I went back to my own console and brought up the visual feed from one of the cameras on the side of the ship. Within the blackness of space was a small, glowing area of fluctuating colours. I zoomed in to see the barrier was reacting to something nestled within it. Not violently or spectacularly, like with the Fertillan Guard ship, but with an oscillating glow that pulsated through the changing spectrum of green, blue and red. It created just enough light to reveal an object big enough to be an old colony ship.

"Do you think that could be Eden?" I said.

"I think it could, yes," said Freddi. "Quite possibly."

CHAPTER SEVENTEEN

THE DESCRIPTION OF Eden contained in the memory ball matched the long, fat shape of the colony ship in front of us. Surrounding the central hub, and connected via five spurs, were five hemispheres where the scientists had planned to grow their hybrid food. The hemispheres were like the agro-domes back on Fertilla, except each one was designed to have a harsh environment like one of the worlds in the Obsidian Rim where the population struggled to grow crops.

Every few moments, as we watched on the monitors, tiny sparks of colour flared out from where the craft made contact with the barrier. It didn't make sense why it was there. Maybe the ship had tried to break back through to our galaxy and got stuck. Maybe its systems had failed and it had drifted in space until it became tangled in the barrier. There was no way to tell from where we were and, with communications impossible with so much interference, the only way to find out was to go over there ourselves.

Access to Eden's shuttle bay was possible by transmitting a code to a receiver on the outside of the hull. The code was included in the information on the memory ball, but transmitting it without it getting scrambled by interference would require getting really close. It would necessitate a really good pilot at the controls of the shuttle and my first choice was Freddi. But he wanted to stay on the ship and manually assess any damage to the systems while also starting the search for the tracker. By the look on his face, it was a request that I dare not countermand. That left the piloting duties down to me. Keya and Terri were so insistent on making the inaugural trip across to Eden that it was impossible to dissuade them from coming. Which left only Stephen who, as he pointed out, was the only bone fide military man among all of us. If he could do nothing else, he could at least shoot straight and I agreed that having him by my side with an EEW would be useful if we encountered anything hostile.

So it was that four of us boarded the shuttle and headed for Eden.

Flying the craft relying completely on visual feeds from the external cameras was nerve-wracking. At least I had been taught by the best – Freddi, who had learnt through trial and error piloting some seriously dilapidated craft in his pirate days. I missed his guiding presence next to me, but Stephen sat in my usual space in the co-pilot's seat and turned out to be invaluable in keeping an eye on the visual feeds in case I missed anything.

As we moved in close to the hull, the nonsense readings from the ship's sensors started to make some kind of sense and I realised that the sheer bulk of the old colony ship was acting as some kind of shield against the worst of the interference.

I transmitted the code and the airlock responded by slowly opening the hatchway to the shuttle bay.

It encouraged me to try communications. "Hello, Eden, this is Captain Cassandra on the shuttle craft about to board with your permission."

Only static replied.

"Hello, Eden, this is the shuttle craft about to board. Please respond."

Again, nothing.

The airlock was fully open. I manoeuvred the shuttle so its headlight shone into the void. It showed an empty space large enough for us to set down. I gently teased power from the engines, watched the visual feeds on my screen to make sure I didn't scrape the sides of the opening, and eased us inside.

Internal lights sensed our presence and illuminated the bay to reveal one single craft was already on board – Eden's own shuttle, I presumed. I lined up my shuttle next to it and brought it in to land as the airlock door closed behind us.

I engaged communications as we waited for the bay to repressurise. "This is shuttle craft to Eden. We have successfully landed in your shuttle bay."

Still no response.

"This is Captain Cassandra on board the shuttle craft in your bay. Would be good to hear from you, Eden."

I shook my head as I waited for a reply and heard nothing.

"It could be there is too much interference for communications to work," said Stephen. "Even inside."

"Or it could be that there's no one listening," I said.

Stephen called up the data at the co-pilot's position and

watched as the shuttle's sensors monitored the outside atmosphere. "According to this, life-support systems are operational," he said. "There is adequate heat and breathable air."

"I'm not going to risk my life on those readings," I said. "We go out in spacesuits until we're sure it's safe."

"Agreed," he said.

Terri and Keya protested that they wanted to go too, but I made them wait in the shuttle. With an EEW each, just in case.

Stephen and I suited up, armed ourselves and stepped out into the shuttle bay.

It was like being in the shuttle bay of almost every other ship I had ever been on. It was basically a large room with an airlock to the outside and a door to the inside. The internal door was not locked and responded to the pressure of my palm on the control, even through my gloved hand.

There was no one to greet us on the other side, only a passageway that stretched out ahead and lit up with automatic lights as we stepped into it.

"Have you been on one of these old colony ships before?" asked Stephen through the suit's communicator. His voice was masked with static interference, but his words were clear.

"A couple of times," I replied. "There's a few in the Rim that people are still living on and they need a lot of repair work. I've been hired to take specialist engineers and replacement parts to them on occasion."

"So you know your way around?"

"Not as such, but the control rooms are usually in the centre to give them maximum protection from anything like hull damage." I looked up ahead at the single corridor which led away from the shuttle bay entrance. "Also, there seems to be only one way to go."

It was an eerie feeling as we started down a succession of passageways and I made a mental note of the direction in which we were travelling. We passed door after door to rooms that were either locked or empty. One of them was someone's personal accommodation with an unmade bed and a few pieces of women's clothing draped over the chair. A fine layer of dust that had settled on every surface suggested no one had been in there for a very long time. The ship's systems should have removed such particles from the air, but with no people around to disturb the atmosphere, the dust ceased to be airborne and, in my experience, could sometimes settle like that.

We found a small crew lounge which could hold a maximum of fifteen people. It was zoned into an area of comfortable seating and an area with tables for eating at. There was no layer of dust and the furniture had been pushed around as if people had been in there and not bothered to put it back into an orderly pattern. But it was still impossible to tell if those people had been in as recently as a couple of hours ago or as long ago as a couple of years.

The control room was our next discovery and, like the rest of the ship, was devoid of any crew.

It was almost double the size of the control room on my ship and was dominated by a wall filled with banks of indicators with tiny lights which displayed green, amber or red depending on their status. Beside them was a digital readout with words such as 'moisture', 'temperature', 'sun-equivalent light' and 'season simulation', which suggested they related to the agro-dome hemispheres we saw from space.

The main control panel, the equivalent to the command console back on my ship, was set around a large chair in the centre.

While I was used to having two screens to monitor different aspects of the ship, this station had just the one screen. But it was huge and curved around the chair in a semi-circle like some sort of amphitheatre. Impressive, but potentially a problem if it malfunctioned because it wouldn't be easy to replace.

Remembering the words of Doctor Robbi Harrist, that they 'made things to last' in the days of the colony ship, I swiped my hand across the screen in an attempt to bring it to life. It didn't respond.

Stephen watched from behind me. "It might need you to touch it with bare skin," he said over the communicator.

I unfastened the seal around the wrist of one hand and pulled off my glove. A suit-pressure warning alarm screamed within my helmet, but I ignored it as I ran my fingers across the screen.

This time, it came to life like it had never been dormant. The full schematic of the ship's systems appeared in front of me in a mass of data that detailed every part of the vessel. The amount of information was overwhelming, but there was one panel in the centre which listed the most important readings, including the ship's environmental controls. All of which were at optimal levels.

Putting my hands on either side of my helmet where it was connected to the rest of the suit, I unclipped the fastenings, twisted it free and exposed my head to the ship's atmosphere. I took a tentative breath of the air inside the control room and my lungs calmly accepted its optimal mix of oxygen and nitrogen.

Stephen's blue eyes watched me through his visor and, seeing that I suffered no ill effects, he took his helmet off too.

"Doesn't look like anyone is on board," he said. His voice sounded much clearer without the filter of the communicator.

"No," I said. My eyes scanned the screen in front of me, looking for a method of scanning for life signs. But, with so much data swimming in front of my eyes, I couldn't see if there was a way of doing that.

"Do you think they're all dead or they abandoned the ship?"

"Could be either," I said. "Or both."

I fiddled about with the screen a little bit more, brought up a lot of pages of data and graphs which meant nothing to me, and eventually stumbled on a map of the whole ship. The cross section showed the inner core with the five hemispheres reaching out on the end of spurs like the four legs and a tail of a strange animal. They were labelled Planetary Environment A, B, C, D and E.

"We need to explore those," I said, pointing at the hemispheres.

Stephen removed his glove and touched the hemisphere marked A. The screen responded to his touch and a schematic of Hemisphere A filled the screen. More data scrolled down the right-hand side while I studied the rudimentary plan which showed the entrance, the dome's environmental control centre and demarcation lines separating out areas for growing different crops. A description at the top read that it mimicked the climate of Silvas with a thin atmosphere, long fifty-hour day and limited heat and light from a distant sun.

"Silvas?" said Stephen. "I don't think I've heard of it."

"Not somewhere I've visited," I said.

"Would you like to visit now?"

I smiled. "Sure."

After copying the image of the main map to my P-tab to make finding our way easier, we left the control room and headed for Hemisphere A.

At the end of a long passageway, we stopped at a locked door operated by a panel at the side. It was very much like the entrances to agro-domes back on Fertilla. I remembered entering a similar door at Freddi's old farm.

With my EEW ready in one hand, I placed my other on the panel. It disengaged the seal with a reluctant sigh, like it hadn't been operated for many years, and opened only a crack before it became stuck.

The smell leaking out from around the opening immediately warned me of something unsavoury beyond. It had the dank, mouldy smell of decay like bodies that had been left to rot.

"If it's the atmosphere of another planet, shouldn't we put on our helmets?" said Stephen.

I checked the atmospheric conditions on my suit. It detected a rise in methane, but nothing dangerous. "I want to see what's in there first." I pushed at the door. Stephen stepped in to help and, between us, we encouraged it to open further.

What we saw was like the old, terrifying footage of once-thriving human colonies destroyed in the Oblivion War. The ground was black from the point it began at the edge of the dome by our feet, to where it ended where the artificial orange sky seemed to come down to meet it on the other side. The occasional black sticks of what was left of tall vegetation rose up from the earth like the ghosts of plants haunting the place where they used to live.

The smell of death was so potent that I instinctively started to breathe through my mouth. Only to taste its rank mouldiness on my tongue.

"My Deity," said Stephen under his breath.

If Hemisphere A had been an experiment to grow food on a planet like Silvas, then it had failed.

I placed my hand on the panel by the door. The sound of a grinding motor – which itself appeared to be dying – struggled to bring the door to a close. The seals clicked into place and the acrid smell of decay began to dissipate.

"Hemisphere B?" said Stephen.

I nodded. "Yeah."

Again we followed the map and, again, we walked down a long passageway to a locked door which separated the ship from the simulated atmosphere of another world.

I placed my hand on the panel and the door released its seal without hesitation. It glided open and a growing shaft of light shone out from the aperture like the brightness of a sun in tight orbit rising above the horizon at the start of a new day. I turned away as the light approached my face and felt its burning heat on my skin and a wave of scorching hot air blow over us.

Next to me, Stephen put on his helmet. I checked the atmospheric conditions and it was registering only oxygen and inert gases. I didn't see the need to fully suit up until I saw Stephen's visor darken in reaction to the light and I understood what he was doing. I secured my helmet too, and the glove I had earlier removed from my hand, and let the suit's controls regulate the temperature around my body. My visor darkened and I turned to look into the world of Hemisphere B.

It was filled with green.

Fronds of plants reached out from the ground with bristle-like leaves that emerged from the stems in rows of sharp spines that tangled with the branches of neighbouring plants to create a thicket of vegetation. They reminded me a little of the straggly native plants that clung to the surface of Fertilla, except they were much bigger and more vigorous. There were so many that it was difficult to see where one plant finished and another plant began. Most of them reached up to around the height of my knee or waist, although some were as tall as Stephen and cast harsh shadows under the intense yellowish white of the dome's sky.

"Extraordinary," said Stephen over the communicator.

"Yeah."

At our feet, there was a narrow strip where the plants seemed not to grow, but to reach in from the side with their branches as if to take advantage of the light and air there. It could have been an illusion, but it looked to me like it might be some sort of path.

"What do you think?" I said. "Shall we go in?"

"I thought that was the plan."

I didn't reply with words, but lifted my EEW so it was ready to fire if I needed to, and stepped inside.

The change from the solid floor of a spaceship to the uneven surface of a pretend planet was distinct and my foot seemed to sink a little into the mix of soil and vegetation. Within a few steps, I was entirely encompassed by the green and hoped that my memory, and the rough outline of a path, was enough for us to find our way back. I was so concentrating on our route that I didn't see something large and heavy heading straight towards me before it bashed me on the head. I swung round and aimed my EEW only to find myself looking directly at a large bulbous fruit hanging down from one of the branches.

Stephen's laugh came over the communicator.

I glared at him, even though he couldn't see my expression through the darkened visor. "I suppose you think that's funny!"

He stifled his laughter. "Not at all, Cassy."

I briefly muted the communicator as I chuckled to myself. If the only danger we were going to meet was hanging fruit, then stalking about with my EEW drawn was a bit overkill. Not that I would ever be without it.

It was only a few metres in before the greenery thinned out a bit and we found ourselves standing on the edge of what was almost certainly a path. It was a walkway of compact soil that stretched from one side of the dome to the other with tributaries coming off it that wound their way through the middle of more blocks, or fields, of vegetation. Each one of the fields had their own characteristics. In one area, the plants reached up to knee height with grass-like tufts of seed on the ends of spiky shoots. In another, they were waist height with green, elongated packets growing off them that weighed the plants down so they appeared to be nodding with fatigue. In a third, tall shoots reached high into the air while round, ball-like protrusions hugged the ground at their roots. They were all different, but they all had a similarity to Fertillan native plants. Like human children with different personalities who still resemble their parents.

I remembered the map of Hemisphere A that Stephen had brought up in the control room. Although this was Hemisphere B, the lines of the separated fields were similar. They reminded me of how Freddi's daughters grew crops on their farm, in specialist areas where one type of food could be easily harvested without it getting muddled with the others. This hemisphere was not as regimented as the agro-domes on Fertilla because in each field there seemed to be rogue species growing among the crops, but there was definitely the evidence of human design.

Something flashed at the corner of my vision – white and fast like a shooting star. I swung towards it, but found myself facing only the field of waist-high nodding plants.

"Did you see that?" I asked over the communicator.

"See what?" said Stephen.

I cursed the restrictions of the helmet. It confined what I could see to an area directly in front of me and a little on either side. It also did a poor job of transmitting sound.

I looked across the hemisphere, with its sea of green extending to the edge and bright domed ceiling above. All seemed still apart from the occasional wavering of the branches as the plants were blown by an artificial breeze around us.

Then I saw it again. The nodding crops swayed like something was among them and a white shape moved through the branches.

"Something's in here with us," I said. "Come on!"

I charged into the field with my EEW ready and Stephen behind me.

The crops buffeted around us as we careered through them; swiping them out of the way with our arms and trampling their stalks underfoot. Ahead of us, branches swayed like someone – or something – was doing the same as us.

I stumbled and recovered my balance a couple of times, only to fall flat on my belly as my feet got tangled in a tough, spindly branch which I didn't see was growing across my path. Almost immediately I was down, I felt Stephen grab my arm and pull me back to standing.

He pointed ahead. "This way!"

I followed the trail of swishing branches and broke into a run.

The mass of green ahead was thinning as we approached the edge of the dome, and the flash of white bobbing up and down between the branches was becoming easier to see. Whatever it was, it was swift and must have been more efficient at moving through the field than we were, but it was running out of room. As I closed in, I swear I saw the swinging arms and running legs of a person.

I stopped sharp at the edge of the dome before I ran into its hard surface. The arch of the glowing sky didn't reach all the way to the ground, but connected with a metre-high rim of black that ran all the way around the bottom of the hemisphere. It was smeared with the green of some sort of growing organism that disguised its presence until I was standing right next to it.

A shrivelled-looking man with white straggly hair down to the top of his shoulders stood with his back to the dome's edge. He was hunched over and naked, apart from a dirty-white loincloth wrapped around his genitals, and his skin was dark and wrinkled. He held a large curved machete in one hand which looked sharp enough to cut me in two and, in the other, one of the elongated packets picked from the nodding crops. He waved both at me threateningly and yelled an angry cry which the microphones in my helmet had no trouble in relaying.

Stephen stepped out of the field on the other side of him.

The man waved his weapons at Stephen and screamed angrily.

"You keep an eye on that blade," I told Stephen as I reached to take off my helmet.

"Cassy, what are you going to do?"

But I had no time to reply before the seals were uncoupled and communications were cut off. I removed my helmet and a rush of hot, stifling air surrounded my face, allowing me to breathe in the dome's air which was sweet with oxygen and the smell of raw vegetables.

The man stared at me with wide eyes.

"It's okay," I said, putting my EEW in the holster strapped to my thigh and holding up my palms in what I hoped was an unthreatening gesture. "We're not going to hurt you."

"*Aaarrrr! Aaarrrr!*" He waved the machete at me and I heard the sharpness of its blade swipe through the air.

"We came in a spaceship to find you."

"*Dead!*" He cowered back against the side of the dome. "*Deeead!*"

"You're not going to die." I took a step forward. His wide-eyed stare became wider. "We're here to help you. Let me help you."

On my second step, he thrust forward and brought the machete swiping down towards me. I jumped back as Stephen lunged forward and grabbed his wrist. With the efficiency of a trained professional, he pushed the man back to the edge of the dome and smashed his hand against the surface several times until the blade was knocked out of his hand.

I picked up the machete and threw it out of reach into the field of crops.

Stephen let go of the man and he slid, weakly, down the side of the dome until his bottom hit the ground. He let go of the vegetable, if that's what it was, and it rolled away.

I squatted down beside him. "That's better," I said. "We don't want to hurt you, we just want to talk."

He lifted his head and looked directly at me like he didn't understand my language. He opened his mouth to say something, but uttered only an unintelligible sound before his eyes glazed over and he passed out.

CHAPTER EIGHTEEN

T HE MAN WOKE up when we carried him into the crew lounge and began ranting incoherently about someone being dead. He seemed confused to the point of madness. He begged us to kill him and then pleaded with us to spare him, all within the space of one breath. He struggled to get free at first, then all of a sudden burst into tears and was inconsolable.

We laid him down on one of the couches and he slipped off it and sat on the floor with his back leaning against it and his head buried in his knees. He seemed to prefer it like that so we left him.

I made an attempt to communicate with the shuttle, but there was too much interference and I sent Stephen off to fetch Keya and Terri while I watched the old man from a distance. When they arrived back, it was all I could do to stop Terri rushing up to him.

"Hey hey, not so fast," I said as I stepped in her way. "He's really scared of people. He might have been living here alone for a long time. You need to be gentle."

While I was dealing with Terri, Keya walked straight past us. I was about to call her back when I saw the man lift his head at the sound of her approaching footsteps. Out of all of us, she was the one who appeared the least threatening in her smart clothes, neat make-up and her relatively petite stature. She was sympathetic at heart and it made sense for her to be the one to try to talk to him.

The man covered his chest with his arms and, for the first time, seemed shy of his semi-nakedness. He was also shivering. The environment we had brought him from was intensely hot, whereas the crew lounge was ambient temperature for humans.

"Cassy," she whispered just loud enough for me to hear. "Can you find a blanket or something?"

I went back to the woman's room that I had encountered on our initial exploration of the ship and pulled one of the covers off the bed. When I returned, Keya was sitting next to the man on the floor and talking to him in subdued tones. She took the cover and wrapped it around his shoulders. He grasped hold of either end and pulled the cover tightly around his body.

"Thank you," he said. It was the first coherent thing I had heard him say.

I withdrew to the other end of the lounge where Stephen had persuaded Terri to sit down at one of the tables.

It was another half an hour before Keya finished talking to the man and joined us.

"You were right, Cassy," she said. "He's been living on this ship on his own for up to twenty years. He's finding communication with people difficult after all this time."

"Who is he?" Terri butted in. "What happened to everyone else?"

"His name is Malcon and he's a descendant from the original crew as you thought," said Keya. "But he's the last one. The others gradually died out and were buried somewhere in one of the hemispheres. They had hoped to have more children so later generations could continue their work, but the women found it increasingly difficult to get pregnant. He's a little hazy on the details, but it seems their proximity to the barrier may have caused fertility problems."

"Poor man," said Terri.

"If the barrier was having such a bad effect on them, why didn't they move further away?" I said.

"Malcon says the ship uses the forces contained in the field to generate energy. He wasn't sure how it works but he said it is the only energy they have, being so far away from any stars which could generate solar power. The operation was all set up before he was born, and it was controlled by the ship's automatic systems so he couldn't tell me any more than that. Also, I get the sense that by the time Eden's crew realised what was causing the fertility problems, it was too late to do anything about it."

"Would Malcon speak to me?" I asked her.

"I wouldn't risk it," said Keya. "I told him that you weren't a dead member of the crew come back to haunt him, but I don't think he's entirely convinced. This has all been a bit of a shock for him."

"Did you manage to ask him about the food research?" I said.

"I did. He said four of the hemispheres were successful and are still active. As people died off, they gradually let them grow almost wild because they were unable to monitor all of the crops and they didn't need all the food they produced to feed everybody. However, by what Malcon says, all the plants in the hemispheres are successful hybrid crops which are able to survive in inhospitable conditions. Malcon likes Hemisphere B because it's warm and has a breathable atmosphere."

"That's amazing, Keya," I said. "You've really found the holy grail."

"Well, according to the testimony of a slightly mad, semi-naked man, yeah. I'd like to take a look myself and study some of the scientific journals, which I believe are kept safe in the ship's systems, but it looks like it."

"You don't sound that excited," observed Stephen.

"It's difficult after listening to Malcon's story," she said. She glanced back at where he had wrapped the bedcover completely around his body and huddled up into a ball. "He's spent half his life wandering around the hemispheres on his own and talking to plants that won't talk back. It's utterly tragic."

WE DISCOVERED THE old laboratory where the scientists on Eden had conducted their food research, much to the excitement of Keya and Terri. From the mess left behind, it looked like the lab had been abandoned for many years. There was layer of dust over everything. It was as if the people who had worked there walked out one day, closed the door and never went back.

The propagation rooms, like the light-filled plant bank Keya had been so proud of back in the underground lab on Fertilla, were empty and their systems had been switched off. None of the scientific equipment in the lab had been touched in as much as a generation and, although it should have been in working order in theory, it would all need to be re-calibrated and checked.

I found Keya hunched over a computer screen embedded into a dusty desk at the near side of the lab. Beside her was a pile of vegetation that had started to wilt from being picked and removed from its habitat in one of the hemispheres. She was so engrossed that she didn't hear me come in and jumped almost out of her seat when my shadow fell across her face and she realised I was standing right next to her.

"Cassy! Don't you knock?"

"Sorry," I said. I looked around to double check she was the only one there. "Where's Terri?"

"I sent her off into the hemispheres to catalogue the plants. When she's in here, she keeps looking up the details of the dead crew and staring at them for hours. I can't imagine what it must be like to wake up and find out everyone you had ever known is dead."

"What about you? You looked engrossed when I came in."

Keya sat back in her chair with a long sigh. "Everything is so fascinating, I don't know where to start."

I looked over her shoulder at the image on the screen. It was a pattern of green, almost hexagonal shapes which were distorted as they bunched in together. "What's that?" I said.

"It's the cells of a Fertillan green bean," said Keya. "The microscope is one of the pieces of lab equipment that seems to be working okay."

She went over to the device which was sitting on a bench at the side of the lab. It was a beast of a machine which was twice as wide as she was and dominated by a central, fat cylindrical column which reached up above her head. She pressed a concealed button on the base, a tray slid out next to her hand and the image on the screen turned to a blank grey. She picked up something from the tray which was so small I couldn't see what it was and she brought it back over to me.

Keya placed the specimen in my hand and I saw it was a piece of vegetation about the size of my thumbnail and slightly curved like a pod of an ordinary green bean which had been cut in half lengthways. With my bare eyesight, I couldn't see any of the cell structure which the microscope had revealed.

"Have you been able to work out if the radiation from the barrier is affecting the plants?" I asked her.

"I don't think so. I need to do more work, but my preliminary analysis suggests any effect is likely to be insignificant. We can see just by walking into the hemispheres that the plants are not having trouble reproducing. Unlike the poor people who lived here."

"Then the food they developed here could be grown on some of the more inhospitable places in the Rim?"

"According to the records left by the crew, yes. They tested everything they grew for human consumption and anything that wasn't fit, they simply removed from the hemispheres. They even came up with a series of recipes for what they grew here. The biggest question is how can we take the crops to the rest of the Rim on any kind of scale? Some of the plants reproduce through seeds, but some of the tubers propagate by growing new buds from the main stem or send out shoots which root and create new plants that way. It's effective for the plant, but propagating at scale will be difficult and labour intensive. I'm not sure how we would do it yet. Then, of course, the plants would need to be trialled on real planets and on real colonies, rather than in artificial hemispheres."

"That sounds like a lot of work, Keya, and I don't know how long we're going to stay here. Freddi said before we left that we should hide on this side of the barrier only until we're able to remove the tracker on our ship and when we're sure the Fertillan Guard ship has had enough time to free itself, think that we've fled and leave."

"I think I'd like to stay and work on the viability of bringing the plants from the hemisphere back inside the Rim," she said. "I suspect Terri would like to stay as well, although I'm not sure what we should do about Malcon."

"If we go, there's a chance we won't be able to come back for you. Stephen and I are still wanted fugitives."

"I understand that," she said. "Which is why, before you go, I want you to bring Freddi over in the shuttle. He can take a look at Eden's engines for us so, if you're not able to come back for us, we can be sure of breaking free and coming back through the barrier ourselves. He can also look at the hemispheres and tell me what he thinks as a former farmer. Mine and Terri's experience is all confined to the lab, whereas he has practical experience of looking after and harvesting crops."

"Of course, Keya," I said. "While he's here, I might ask him to cook some of the food grown on Eden. You've not lived if you haven't had a taste of Freddi's cooking."

Keya shook her head as if she hadn't heard me properly. "Freddi?"

"He told me he used to cook for his family sometimes and, when they had labourers on the farm around harvest time, he used to cook for them too. Sometimes, when our ship was hired as a venue for off-world sex parties or business meetings on neutral territory, he would also cook then. In fact, we should have a party."

"A party?"

As soon as I said it, I was excited about the idea. "Why not?" I said. "After all we've been through, we deserve to have some fun."

Keya looked bemused at the concept. "I'm not entirely sure I can remember what fun is like."

"Exactly!" I said. "Let's call it a celebration: a big party to celebrate that we've found Eden and we're still alive."

CHAPTER NINETEEN

THE EXCITEMENT IN Freddi's eyes when I suggested he create a banquet for us all using the food produced on Eden undermined his complaints that he was too busy doing things for Keya. He became even more enthusiastic when she showed him the recipes she had found stored on the computer. He spent a day gathering raw food from the hemispheres and another day preparing it in Eden's kitchen.

As evening approached, we all gathered in the crew lounge for the party and that's when I realised Terri was missing. The others had gone to persuade Malcon to join us and I thought that's where she might still be, except that I found Malcon sitting on the floor in between two pieces of comfortable furniture which provided him with some sort of hideaway from the rest of us. He said Terri had been asking him what had happened to the crew when they died and he told her they had been buried in Hemisphere D. Malcon explained the bacteria in the soil would break down their bodies until they became part of the earth and fertilised the very vegetation they had planted there when they were alive. Terri, it seemed, had decided that rather than spend time partying with the living, she would visit the dead.

I went to find her in Hemisphere D.

The dome lay at the end of a long corridor which ran down the inside of one of the spurs of Eden and, like all of the hemispheres, was entered by way of an airtight door.

Outside this particular airtight door was a row of thick, padded coats hanging up on hooks with corresponding pairs of boots lined up underneath. There were five hooks and four sets of coats and boots which made me almost certain that Terri was wearing the missing set.

I kicked off my normal boots, put on the warm ones, and slipped my arms into the coat. There was a second row of hooks on the other side of the door which contained several sets of breathers. I grabbed one of them before I put my hand on the control panel to go inside.

The door slid open to reveal a white, frosted landscape. The thin layer of ice spread out across the surface of the hemisphere until it touched the boundary wall that curved around the edge of the environment. Sticking up from the ground, and also covered in a layer of frost, were the scraggy leaves of plants which hugged the soil in a carpet of frozen green that reached no higher than my calf. Above them arched the dark grey of the dome which looked like the underside of a cloudy sky on a planet either a long way from its sun or experiencing the twilight of evening.

I stepped out into the simulated world and my foot crunched on the ice. The door closed automatically behind me to keep the atmosphere inside and I understood why it had been necessary to have the coats hanging ready to be used. The icy air went straight through my shirt and prickled my skin. I fumbled with the coat's zip, as my fingers were already cold enough to be stiff, but managed to do it up and seal my body heat inside. I was also having trouble breathing the air which, despite having some oxygen in it, was very thin. I put the breather over my face, turned on the air supply and sucked in deep. Tucking the air tank under my arm, rather than fiddling with the harness to secure it to my back, I thrust my hands into my pockets and I found a pair of thick gloves which I was suddenly very grateful for.

The hemisphere was so wide and its vegetation so short and spindly that it was a little unnerving to be in such an open space. But it had the advantage that it enabled me to see if anyone else was in there and, almost immediately, I spotted Terri standing alone off to one side. I walked over to join her, with my feet crunching with each step and leaving the mark of my footsteps in the frost.

Terri stood in quiet contemplation, looking down at the frozen ground. She must have sensed me approach, but she didn't speak, turn to look at me or move in any way.

"Terri, what are you doing here?" I said, my voice muffled by the breather mask. "Freddi's about to serve up his meal. You can't miss it, he's been cooking all day."

She continued to stare at the ground. "Malcon isn't quite sure where they're buried," she said, eventually.

"The crew?"

"And their children and their children's children. He said their graves are definitely in Hemisphere D, but he could only tell me they were 'somewhere to the left of the middle'. He said they used to be obvious because you could see where the ground had been disturbed, but the plants grew over the graves eventually and now it's impossible to tell."

"Does it matter exactly where?" I said.

"I suppose not, but I wanted to visit them to pay my respects."

"I'm sure if they were looking down on you, they wouldn't mind if you were standing slightly in the wrong place."

"Do you believe in that, Cassy?"

"Believe in what?"

"That the dead are looking down on us?"

"No," I said. "But sometimes it's nice to pretend they are. I sometimes hope that, if my mother was looking down on me, she wouldn't be too horrified at the life I'm leading."

Terri went quiet. She lifted her head and looked out across the landscape. Frozen, yet still alive. "These plants grow their food underground, did Keya tell you?"

"I think she mentioned it."

"The tubers are protected in the soil. Some of them even need the frost to turn their starch into sugars so they don't taste bitter. It's amazing, isn't it?"

"Yes it is," I said.

"These people achieved that." She pointed at the ground. "These people buried here. They gave up their lives and their homes to come here to do this amazing thing and if we hadn't found them, it would all have been lost forever."

"The important thing is, we did find them. Thanks to your father ensuring that the secret of Eden's location didn't die with him."

"I knew some of these people. At least, I knew some of the original crew. I found their details in the ship's manifest and looked at their pictures and tried to remember how they moved and talked. I came such a long way and all I've found are their graves – and I can't even locate them properly."

"Malcon survived," I said.

"I know. He's still not quite what I imagined," she said.

"Don't be too hard on Malcon. He's been through a lot too." I looked up at the dark grey of the dome's artificial sky. It seemed to have got darker since I walked in, as the twilight of evening was turning to the black of night. "There's something else you could do to honour the memory of the people who are buried here. You could come back to the crew lounge with me and eat some of the food they learnt to grow."

Terri sighed and the moisture in her breath clouded the mask of her breather. "I'm not sure I want to."

"The thing is, I was the one who persuaded Freddi to do the cooking in the first place and if we don't turn up to eat, I'll never hear the end of it."

For a moment, I thought she wasn't going to come back with me, but then a massive shiver ran through her body and it seemed to remind her how cold it was in Hemisphere D. "Okay," she said. "I'll come if you want me to."

She turned away from where the graves of the dead Eden crew might have been and I followed her back towards the entrance, with both our pairs of boots crunching in the frost.

I HAD NEVER seen so much food. Freddi had laid it all out on one of the tables in the crew lounge in a display large enough for us to feast on twice over. In the centre was a steaming vegetable stew in some sort of dark red sauce or gravy. Surrounding it were a plate of baked orange-coloured tubers, a salad of multi-coloured vegetables mixed with cooked grain, a pile of vegetables which had been fried until crispy, and a stack of little flatbreads which Freddi had made after persuading Keya to hand-grind a grain crop to make some sort of flour. It looked amazing and smelled even better.

When Terri and I returned from Hemisphere D, I saw that Stephen had already piled up a plate with a selection of everything and was carrying it away from the table. It was only when he walked straight past me to the back of the lounge that I realised it was not for himself, but for Malcon who remained in his little hideaway between the comfortable furniture. At least he had taken to wearing a shirt and trousers in our presence, although he didn't look very comfortable in proper clothes and kept fiddling nervously with the material.

Terri joined Keya in tucking into the feast while Freddi, flushed and sweaty from cooking, watched them with his hands on his hips and an expression of satisfaction on his face.

"Looks amazing, Freddi," I said, as I walked up to him.

"Thanks, Cassy."

I grabbed a couple of empty plates from a stack on the side of the table and passed one to him. "Are you going to stand there looking at it for the rest of the evening, or are you actually going to eat some?"

He took the plate from me. "I'm game, if you are."

Freddi started modestly by picking up a couple of the flat-breads and putting them on his plate while I helped myself to a large spoonful of the red stew. As I returned the serving spoon to the bowl, I looked up to see Stephen coming back from the comfortable seating area carrying two large bottles of pale yellow liquid.

"It turns out Malcon makes his own wine," he said, placing the bottles down on the table. "He wants us to have these as a sort of a thank you."

I looked at them suspiciously. "Is it drinkable?"

"Malcon drinks it," he replied.

"That's not necessarily a recommendation," I said.

Nevertheless, when some mugs were handed out, I allowed a little bit of the wine to be poured into mine. I tried a cautious sip and was rewarded – if that was the right word – with the sting of sour and bitter flavours that lingered on my tongue while the alcohol warmed my throat. The sensation was almost pleasant and so I decided to pour myself a little bit more. It contrasted well with the sweet and savoury flavours of Freddi's cooking and I lost track of how much I drank. By the sound of the loud voices and laughter around me, I wasn't the only one.

Freddi came over to sit down next to me as I was scraping up the last bit of the red sauce from my plate with my final piece of flatbread. At one of the other tables, Stephen and Keya were engaged in an intense argument about Fertilla's ruling system which Terri was watching by turning her head to look between the two speakers like it was some kind of ball game.

"I've been meaning to tell you," said Freddi. "Before I left the ship, I found the tracker that the Fertillan Guard hid on board."

"You found it? Where?"

"Hidden in the communications array. Their technicians had hooked it up to our systems to give the signal a boost. The bastards."

"So they can't track us now?"

"They can't track us now."

"Which begs the question, where do we go from here?" I said.

"Anywhere without links to Fertilla."

"With their stranglehold on controlling the food supply, that doesn't leave us with too many places."

"I'll draw up a list," said Freddi.

Stephen's laughter suddenly erupted from the conversation he was having and Keya and Terri responded with tipsy giggles.

"How long until you think it's safe to leave?" I said.

"A few more days. I still need to look at Eden's engines for Keya, but I'm worried I won't be able to test them while the ship is tied into the barrier and I don't know enough about how it generates energy to risk moving the ship away. I think she's crazy to want to stay here, and I told her so. But she kept going on about how Eden is the scientific discovery of a lifetime and there was no persuading her otherwise."

"Is Malcon staying?" I asked.

"I think so. Keya and Terri can look after him here and there's nowhere I can think of where he'd be safe. A farm on Fertilla, possibly, but we can't go back while you're still wanted for treason."

"No," I said in contemplation at our lack of options.

Freddi nodded across the other side of the room to where Stephen had apparently finished his conversation with Keya and Terri and was standing by the buffet table, topping up his mug with more of Malcon's potent home brew. He held the bottle up to the light to see how much was left – it appeared to be almost half empty – and started walking in our direction.

"I'm going to make a start on clearing up," said Freddi, getting off his chair.

"You can do that tomorrow," I protested.

But Freddi was already on his feet. "You two need to talk," was all he said before he walked away.

"Where's Freddi off to?" said Stephen as he reached where we were sitting. "I was going to see if he wanted any more wine before Keya drinks it all."

Keya had returned to the buffet table and was picking through some of the last of the food while swaying a little in her sensible shoes. Either she had had most of the bottle that Stephen had brought over, or she wasn't used to drinking alcohol.

"Freddi says we should talk," I said.

"Ah," said Stephen, sitting down on the chair vacated by Freddi. "Talk about what?"

I shrugged. "I don't know. Us, I suppose. The future."

"He's right that we have some decisions to make."

"Yes." I avoided looking Stephen in the eye and stared down into what was left of my mug of wine. I swirled the dribble of liquid and watched as it created a sort of whirlpool in the bottom. "I've been thinking that I can't make Freddi travel with me any longer. There are going to be too many worlds off limits for me after the assassination and that's going to reduce the number of places where we can find freelance jobs. It's unfair on Freddi. He won't even be able to go back to Fertilla to visit his daughters while I'm still with him."

I drained the last of my wine and licked the residue off my lips.

Stephen passed the bottle over to me. "Do you want some more of that?"

"No," I said. I could feel that I was a little drunk already and I was concerned that whatever Malcon did to ferment his wine was going to cause one vac of a hangover in the morning.

"Are you sure?" he said.

"No." The alcohol had taken away a little of my anxiety about our next moves and I liked the way it felt. I removed my hand from over my mug and allowed Stephen to fill it to the brim.

"I've been thinking too." Stephen placed the bottle on the floor and sat back in his chair. "About the promise I made to James."

"I wouldn't worry about honouring any promise made to that man. That man has no honour."

"I promised I would find out who really killed Queen Triana and it's something I still intend to do. It's the only way to clear your name and prevent me from spending the rest of my life in exile."

"The monk shouted 'free Manupia,'" I said. "If that is the cause he was fighting for, then that's where we need to go. But Fertilla has too many close links to Manupia and it's not safe for us."

"I think it could be worth the risk," said Stephen. "My only reservation is a selfish one."

I looked away from my wine and into his face for the first time since he had sat next to me. He returned my gaze and, despite the party going on around us, it seemed like we were the only two people in the room. "Oh?" I said.

"If we clear your name and the King pardons me for breaking an innocent woman out of jail, then I will be expected to return to my position as the head of the Fertillan Guard and I'll no longer be able to travel the galaxy with you."

He leant closer to me until I could feel the warmth radiating from his body and hear the subtle whisper of his breath.

His lips reached mine and I allowed them to linger for a moment before a swell of desire within me compelled me to return the kiss. His hand brushed my cheek and slid through my hair to the back of my head to pull me close. I did not resist and reached round his shoulder to clasp his body to mine. In my other hand, the mug of wine tipped so its cool liquid split onto my lap, but I hardly noticed. There was only me and Stephen, enjoying each other like I had secretly longed to do ever since he greeted me in his dressing room on his fateful wedding day.

We might have sat quietly kissing like that for a long time, but a sudden crash jolted us apart.

I looked up to see Freddi had dropped one of the plates he had been clearing up from the buffet table. He looked down at the broken pieces at his feet, while Keya and Terri looked up from their conversation.

"Do you think he was watching us?" whispered Stephen.

"Possibly," I said and felt my face go red as I realised that he almost certainly was. "But no one's watching us now."

With everyone's attention taken by the broken crockery, and Keya and Terri going over to help Freddi pick up the pieces, I reached out for Stephen's hand and stood up from my chair. He followed my lead and we slipped away from the party, stopping only to place our mugs on a table as we left.

Out in the corridor, I let go of Stephen's hand to break into a run.

"Where are we going?" he called after me.

"To a bed that no one has slept in for a generation," I shouted back.

He chased me through the corridors with his laughter and my giggles echoing around us as the sounds bounced off the ship's walls.

I knew exactly where I was going and followed the turnings that I had memorised on our first arrival on Eden, until we reached the personal accommodation that had once belonged to a female member of the crew.

I grabbed Stephen by the shirt and pulled him inside.

"Should we be in here?" he said, looking around at what had once been somebody's private space.

"Probably not." I giggled.

I knew the wine was partly responsible for breaking down my inhibitions, but I didn't care. I levered myself up onto my tiptoes so my face was level with Stephen's and clasped his head to bring him close to me. My kiss was intense and passionate, and his reaction was fervent and earnest. My tongue teased out his tongue and, as we explored each other, they became entwined like two pieces of yarn twisted to form a single thread.

He tentatively brushed my breast with his fingers and I grabbed them to press his hand back against my nipple to show how desperately I wanted him to touch me. I dropped from my tiptoes and staggered backwards, bringing Stephen with me, until my spine hit the wall. He slipped his hand through the fastening of my shirt and a button pinged off to bounce away under the chair where the woman who used to sleep there had draped a few items of clothing.

I sighed with desire as the naked flesh of Stephen's hand cupped my breast beneath my shirt as if the two pieces of our bodies were made for each other. His breath deepened as I sensed his long-denied passion rising to the surface. I grabbed at the lapels of his jacket and tried to pull them off his shoulders, but I was at the wrong angle and giggled at my own ineptitude as he helped me undress him.

Eagerly, we pulled at each other's clothes – wrestling with buttons, sliding our zips and tugging at fabric – until we stood naked before each other. Sweat glistened between the twisting hairs of his chest and I wanted to hold him close against me. But he paused. He placed his forehead onto my forehead so they were the only parts of our bodies touching. His striking blue eyes looked into mine. "Are you okay about this, Cassy?" he asked.

"Yes, I want to," I whispered.

Suddenly, he was holding my hand and pulling me towards the bed. It no longer had a covering because I had taken it to keep Malcon warm, but we were so hot for each other, it didn't matter. He slid onto the mattress first and I followed, clambering on top of his strong, muscular body and sensing its masculine beauty as I pressed myself against him. We kissed again: longingly, urgently, wildly.

But I wanted more than his tongue inside of me. I wanted him all of him.

We could deny ourselves no longer and made love on the stranger's bed.

It was like all the pain from what his mother had said to me, all the fear from being locked in a Fertillan cell, the panic as people bayed for my blood outside the courtroom, the desperation as we ran from the jail, the subjugation of submitting to cryo-sleep and the risk of double-crossing Everade's guards were all released in one single moment of human passion.

I screamed so loud as the orgasm exploded throughout my body that I drowned out Stephen's cries as he climaxed inside of me.

Even after we finished, I sizzled with the aftershocks and lay clutching onto Stephen's torso like I never wanted to let him go.

I listened to the beating of his heart through the wall of his chest as it gradually slowed to a normal rhythm.

He brushed my fringe from my sweaty forehead and planted a delicate kiss. "I should never have been born a prince," he said.

"Why do you say that?"

He squeezed me tight and I snuggled into him. "I should have been born a spacefarer," he said. "Then the galaxy would never have forced us apart."

I stroked my hand across his pectoral muscles and allowed my fingers to trace a path through his hairs and over the bumps of his ribs. The memory of our intimacy was still firing within me and the sensuality of exploring his body filled me with satisfaction. "If we go to Manupia and clear my name, then the chances are you will become a prince again."

"I know, Cassy. But if we don't go, you won't be free to travel the Rim and I will have to spend my life looking over my shoulder."

"Then we don't have choice, do we?"

"No," he said. "We have to go to Manupia."

We lay there for a long time like that, until the heat of sex had dissipated and we started to feel cold on the bed without a cover.

But our passion hadn't died. It had merely been resting.

So we enjoyed each other's bodies again until the orgasms came, our cries reverberated around the room and we felt more alive than we had ever done before.

CHAPTER TWENTY

TURBULENCE ROCKED THE ship as it emerged from the barrier and hundreds of objects clattered against its hull like giant hailstones.

I looked at my console, but the scrambled field was still making a mess of my readings and the visual feeds remained blank. We were flying blind into the Deity knows what.

"Freddi?" I said.

He stared at his own console and shook his head. "It feels like space debris, but it can't be so far out on the Rim."

A large lump of something struck the outside of the ship above my head and I instinctively ducked. "Whatever this stuff is, that bit almost holed us."

Stephen ran in from the corridor. "What's going on? I thought you said it would be easier coming back through."

"It should be," said Freddi. "I don't know what's causing it."

Static from the visual feeds fizzed on my screen. We were moving further away from the barrier and its powerful interference was weakening. The white and grey noise faded to solid black with floating specks of white and grey. For a moment, I thought the specks were the result of static corrupting the feed, then one of them loomed large as it sped towards us. It filled the screen for a second before it crashed right into the external camera and the image was cut dead.

"You're right, Freddi. It's debris," I said. "Can you steer us away from it?"

"If I can figure out where it's coming from," he said. "These vacking readings are all over the place. I don't want to take the wrong turn and fly any closer than we already are."

Stephen rushed to one of the spare consoles and pulled up visual feeds for himself. "Where's the Fertillan Guard ship?" he said.

"It's been days since we left them," said Freddi. "They would have discovered how to free themselves by now. They should have wormholed away – with us hidden behind the barrier, there was no reason for them to stay."

"Unless they're still stuck," I said.

"Unless they're neither," said Stephen. "Freddi, can you try moving us away from the last known position of the Fertillan Guard ship?"

"I can do that," said Freddi.

He didn't need me to confirm the suggestion, because as soon as Stephen made it, we were all thinking the same thing.

Freddi fired the engines and the ship took a slow and steady path through normal space. The clattering on the hull lessened until we heard and felt nothing. Ellen came back on line and said she would compile a damage report. But we were all focussed on the visual feeds from the remaining external cameras.

Where the Fertillan Guard ship used to be was a collection of jagged and twisted metal. The pieces hung in space like rocks in an asteroid field, many of them still flying away from the forces that had caused the ship to break up in the first place, while others were slowed by the gravity generated by the barrier itself and the mass of the larger pieces of debris so they twirled around each other like miniature star systems.

"What the vac happened?" I said, mesmerised by the image on my screen.

"The barrier must have destroyed them somehow," said Freddi.

"I think they tried to wormhole away while they were still stuck in it," said Stephen.

"The barrier prevents the formation of wormholes," said Freddi. "Everyone knows that."

"Look at the pattern of the debris," said Stephen. "I recognise parts of the front of the ship, but nothing from the rear where the engines were. I think, rather than try to gently extricate himself from the barrier, Everade tried to use the most powerful weapon he had to force himself free. He tried to use the QED, but instead of wrenching himself clear, it backfired and blew him up."

"Drakh," said Freddi.

I pulled up a feed from the camera that should have been pointing right at the Fertillan Guard shuttle. If it had escaped the blast, then there could still be people alive in there.

But it had not been so lucky. A large piece of debris from the main ship looked like it had been blown towards them in the explosion and sheared off the front corner of the vessel which was sticking out of the barrier. Through the gaping hole it had created, it was possible to see the inside of the shuttle, still intact. The pilot was still strapped into their seat with their helmet off. They must have sat in there, watching their own ship explode, and a piece of severed hull speed towards them knowing, in those last few seconds, that they could do nothing to stop it. They would have been conscious when part of the shuttle was wrenched away and their air supply dissipated into space. The liquid on their eyes and tongue would have instantly boiled away and they might briefly have been aware of the pain before they passed out and died of asphyxiation.

It was a horrific death.

As I looked at what was left of the shuttle, I saw the body of one of the Fertillan Guards who must have been ejected in the collision, floating alongside it. It could have been the guard who had cuffed me in my shuttle bay. It could have been the guard who had barked orders at us through the speaker in her helmet. I hadn't known them as people, I hadn't even known their names, but the fact that I had met them made their deaths seem more real.

"We should have told them how to free themselves," said Stephen.

"They wouldn't have listened," said Freddi.

"But we could have tried."

"Ask yourself," said Freddi, "when you were the head of the Fertillan Guard, if someone you were chasing gave you some advice about how to get out of a dangerous situation, would you have believed them?"

Stephen thought for a moment. "I would have not."

"There's nothing you could have done. Everade blew himself up, and took every member of his crew with him. That disastrous mistake is on him and only him."

I swiped away the images of the dead and brought up the readings coming from the ship's sensors. They were still erratic, but the cold, hard numbers gave me something else to concentrate on.

"Freddi, set a course away from here in normal space," I said. "When we're at a safe distance from the barrier, and if Ellen says there is no significant damage to the ship, begin the calculations to wormhole to Manupia."

"Aye aye, Captain."

CHAPTER TWENTY ONE

KEYA HAD TOLD me, before we left her, Terri and Malcon aboard Eden, that we must not fail in our mission to Manupia. If we were killed or captured, we both knew there would be no one left to go back for the three of them. Keya had left details of the location of Eden with Rob in case she didn't return, but both of us knew the dentist was no spacefarer and certainly didn't have the knowledge required to travel through the barrier.

It was her words that were in my mind as we took the shuttle down to Shangi port, the main space hub on the edge of Shangi, the largest of Manupia's industrial cities.

Freddi, despite his reservations, said he would come with us. If I was going to try to find out information about an organisation powerful enough to order an assassination on another planet, then he said I would need him to cover my back. By the way he said it, I sensed he didn't trust Stephen to do a good enough job without a squadron of Fertillan Guard at his command. I had more faith in

Stephen than he did, but Freddi and I had always been a team and knowing he was there to support me made me feel less nervous.

The port, with its grimy smell, residue of grease, subdued lighting and drab colours looked exactly the same as it had on our previous visit, with the obvious exception that there were fewer ships. The shuttles and the larger freight vessels still lined up ready to take goods from the factory planet – as many people called Manupia – there were just fewer of them.

As we walked through it, a woman entering one of the shuttles turned to look at us as she waited for the hatch to fully open. It wasn't the sort of casual glance that people give you because you happen to be moving by, she stared longer and harder than that. Then a man who was loading up some cargo onto a small wheeled vehicle also turned to stare and I had the uncomfortable sense that people were watching us.

As soon as we had passed the man and he had gone back to concentrating on what he was doing, Freddi grabbed Stephen by the sleeve and pulled him behind one of the large freight ships. I followed them into the shadows.

Stephen shook off Freddi's grip and straightened his sleeve. "Is there a problem?" he asked.

"People are recognising you," said Freddi.

Stephen brushed his hand through his hair which had grown enough since we had left Fertilla so that the brown roots were showing and the yellowish blonde bits on the end were starting to look like some sort of fashion statement. "It's this stupid hair. I should have had it cut off."

"It's not your hair," said Freddi. "It's your royal face."

"People don't recognise me outside of the Fertillan system," said Stephen. "I've been to quite a few worlds in Fertillan Guard ships and, people might know my name, but they don't know what I look like."

"That's before you nearly married the sister of the Manupian president."

I put my hand on Stephen's shoulder where Freddi had grabbed hold of his sleeve, but in a more gentle manner. "Perhaps it would be better if you went back to the shuttle," I suggested.

He looked at me with his large, blue eyes and seemed genuinely affronted. "But, Cassy, we need to clear your name."

"We can't do that if people are staring at you because they think you're a prince," I said.

"Let me and Cassy go," said Freddi.

"But you're the one who said it's a crazy idea," Stephen told Freddi.

"We have done crazy stuff together before. We're a team. We can know what each other is thinking with just a look. Two of us are going to attract less attention than three."

"Let us go alone," I said to him. "We'll report back to you. It'll be better this way."

I pulled myself up on my tiptoes and leant forward to kiss him on the cheek. It was a quick, non-sensual kiss, but as I withdrew and allowed my heels to return to solid ground, I saw his face soften and knew it had affected him.

"I'll wait for you in the shuttle, Cassy, if that's what you think is best." He then turned to Freddi. "Make sure you look after her."

"Of course," said Freddi.

Stephen stepped out from the shadow of the freighter and headed back the way we had come.

Freddi watched him go and then turned to me. "Are you two together again?"

I sighed. "I don't know."

"You know that having a relationship with a prince has only got you into trouble in the past."

"Yeah," I said.

"You're going to have to make a decision about him sooner or later. A real decision."

"I know, Freddi."

"Come on," he said, leading me back onto the thoroughfare of the spaceport. "Let's find that beer. I don't know about you, but I could use a drink."

THE BAR WAS on the edge of the spaceport. It was close to the transport station which took people to and from Shangi city itself and acted almost as a gateway between the two. The building was nestled into the corner of the giant hangar which was tall enough to house all the freight vessels and appeared dwarfed by the wall which marked the outer edge of the environmental enclosure.

It was the same bar we had been to on our previous visit to Manupia and we knew it was the sort of place where newcomers asking a few questions would not draw attention. It had the same grimy smell that I remembered, but not everyone had the muscular, rugged look that I associated with spacefarers who had been exposed to different environments as they lugged heavy freight around different colonies in the galaxy. Many of them wore drab-coloured clothes like local people and were thin and pale like factory workers. It was the thin ones who were clustered around the tables to the right side of the door as we walked in. The same ones who looked up and stared at us as we approached the counter. Many of them had bowls in front of them, which they were eating from furiously and defensively as if we were about to swoop on them and steal their food.

Even the barman gave us a strange look when we ordered two pints of beer which was, I thought, not an unusual thing to do in a bar.

Freddi and I took our drinks to one of the available tables on the left side of the door and sat opposite each other.

Freddi leant across his pint and kept his voice low. "I think something's going on," he said.

"That's the impression I'm getting."

I kept my head down while I lifted my eyes to take another look around the bar. One of the clientele – a tall, gaunt man with dirty-looking stubble – caught me watching him and returned my gaze with a penetrating stare. I quickly turned away, but I felt his eyes still on me as I took a mouthful of beer.

"Drakh," I said, as I saw out of the corner of my eye that the man and his shorter companion, with a wild hairstyle sticking out of the top of his head, was approaching our table.

The tall one stood beside my chair and the shorter one stood beside Freddi's so they blocked the way out from either side of the table.

Freddi, completely unfazed by their presence, stared up at the tall one. "If you're looking for somewhere to sit, this table's taken."

"We're not interested in your table," said the man. "We came to take a closer look at your friend."

The man with the wild hairstyle turned his head sideways as he looked at me, as if scrutinising all the features of my face from every angle. I had endured such scrutiny before from drunken spacefarers who thought they could procure me for sex and I had always rebuffed their advances with tough talk, or sometimes a spit in the face or a kick in the balls. But the wild-haired man was looking into my face, not at my breasts as sexual predators tended to do.

"My friend isn't interested in you," Freddi told him.

I was grateful for his chivalry, but I was perfectly capable of batting away the man's advances myself. Nevertheless, I reached for my EEW which was clipped into its holster at my thigh under the table just in case. I didn't want to use it, but it gave me reassurance to know it was there.

"Why don't you leave us to drink our beer quietly, okay?" I suggested.

"I told you it's not her," said the tall one. "This one's got short hair."

"Of course it's her!" insisted his wild-haired companion.

I was about to ask what the vac they were talking about when a petite woman barged through from behind them and virtually launched herself against the table. "Sheri!" she cried when she saw me.

I was so taken aback, that when she leant forward and engulfed me in a massive hug like I was a long lost friend, I allowed her to do it.

'Sheri' had been the undercover name I had used when I was last on Manupia and the woman looked familiar. As she hugged me, she rested her chin on my shoulder so her mouth was close to my ear. "It's not safe here," she whispered.

She released her embrace, but still hung onto my shoulders and looked at me at arm's length with small, intense eyes. It gave me a chance to recognise her. She had been one of the people that my contact, Mel, had helped to get out of the factories with the promise of a new life on another planet. She was much younger than me, somewhat timid, and had chickened out of leaving at the last minute. While the rest of us had deigned to be smuggled on board a spaceship to freedom, she had become scared and run off back to the factory. Quite sensibly, as it turned out, because out of the four of us who left Manupia on that day, I was the only one who was still alive.

"Denni?" I said, remembering her name.

"Oh Sheri, it's so good to see you!" she said, with loud exuberance. "It's been *so* long since we were at the factory together." She grabbed my hand. "Come with me, I need to show you something."

I found myself being hauled up from the table. I glanced back at Freddi in a way which I hoped showed it was okay for me to go with this woman, and I just caught a hint of his worried expression before Denni squeezed past the two men and pulled me with her. I thought she would let go of my hand at that point, but she kept going and led me back to the front door and out onto the street.

Suddenly away from people, I tugged my hand free. "Denni, what's going on?"

"We can talk down here." She nodded along the path.

The corner of where the bar met the external wall of the hangar was darker than the rest of the street, as it lay on the edge of where the beams of the overhead lights could practically reach. There were bits and pieces of rubbish all around the corner from where they had drifted in from the well-trodden path of the street cleaners, or possibly where others had dropped litter while gathering in the corner to carry out shady dealings.

"What are you doing back here?" said Denni. She leant against the wall so she had a full view of the street behind my shoulder. I tried to shift my stance so I didn't entirely have my back to the bar.

"It's complicated," I said. I didn't have time for an explanation and, although I was grateful to her for pulling me away from those men, I didn't owe her anything.

"The reports say your name's not really Sheri. They say it's Sesaan Cassandra."

I suddenly felt less safe. She knew more about me than I had told her. "Reports?"

"The assassination reports," she said, like it was obvious. "You were the one who opened fire at the wedding. I recognised you as soon as I saw them. I said, that's Sheri who used to work at the factory, but nobody took any notice of me."

I felt the blood drain from my skin as I started to suspect why we had received so much attention since we stepped out of the shuttle. "Tell me about these reports," I asked, fearing I already knew the answer.

"Haven't you seen them?" said Denni, reaching into her pocket for her P-tab. "I thought everyone had seen them. Perhaps you weren't able to when you were in jail."

She showed me the screen of her P-tab and my stomach tightened as I saw an image of myself stepping into the courtroom back on Fertilla with my hands cuffed in front of me. The bruising around my eye was an ugly brown and purple, my long hair was dishevelled and I was wearing the blue dress from the wedding which looked totally inappropriate for my surroundings and my predicament. As the footage continued to play, it cut to the judge who read out the charges against me and I experienced the same frisson of dread that I remembered from when I had stood there for real. Then the footage cut back to me in the dock as I turned in desperation to the people assembled in the court. "Free Manupia!" I shouted. The guard pulled me away and the report ended.

Denni put her P-tab back in her pocket and was grinning when she looked back up at me.

"That's the report?" I said, horrified at what I had seen. "That's the *full* report?"

"Of course it is."

"What about everything else I said?"

But Denni wasn't listening. "Everyone's so proud of you! You knew what was going on at the factories, and even though you escaped, you didn't forget us. You stopped the president's sister getting married to that Fertillan prince and saved the people of Manupia – you're a hero."

CHAPTER TWENTY TWO

I SAW DENNI'S EYES focus on something behind me and, hearing
footsteps, I whipped round to see who it was.

It was Freddi. He had exited the bar and was walking towards
us.

"Cassy, are you all right?" he asked.

It was a relief to see him.

"Who is this?" said Denni.

"This is Freddi, my friend," I said. "He helped me escape from
jail."

It wasn't strictly true, but it was a useful shortcut to say that I
trusted him with my life.

"Then I am pleased to meet you." She reached out a hand and
Freddi accepted the handshake while looking somewhat bemused.

"Cassy, what's going on?"

"This is Denni," I said, trying to explain as much as I
could without letting on that I didn't know very much myself.

"I met her while I was working undercover at the factory."

"What's a factory worker doing out here in a bar for spacefarers?" he said.

"I'm workless now," said Denni. "They were cutting back on staff and they let me go."

"So you're out at the spaceport looking for work?" suggested Freddi.

"No, I…" She looked across at me as if to ask if she should continue. I nodded that she could. "Some of the workless have been coming out here because the Free Manupia movement has been providing food for us. It's better than meeting in the centre of the city."

"You told me in there it wasn't safe," I said.

"Not all the workless are loyal to Free Manupia. It's possible that one of them could report seeing The Assassin to the security services. We also think that someone from the security services could be trying to infiltrate our group out here. This used to be a good recruiting ground for members, but we have to be careful now. I've been trying to vet people when I meet them, but it's not easy."

"The Assassin?" said Freddi.

"Yes," said Denni, evidently completely misinterpreting the question. "Chrisov is going to be so excited that you're here. I assume you'll want to meet him? He sure as vac will want to meet you."

She pulled out her P-tab again as Freddi gave me a questioning look. I shook my head as if to say it was all too complicated and I would explain later.

"I know someone with access to a private transport who can take us to Chrisov," she said as she flicked through several screens on her P-tab. "You can't take a public transport into the city, you're too recognisable."

"I'm sorry," I said. "Who is Chrisov?"

Denni looked at me in disbelief. "You don't know?"

"Like you say, I've been in jail and on the run."

"Of course! Chrisov is… well, he organises things around here. I expect you knew him when you were here before by a codename or something."

"Yes," I said, throwing an uncertain glance over to Freddi. "I expect so."

"This is going to be fabulous," she said. "I told Chrisov that I had worked with you in the Jonsonii factory, but he didn't believe me. Now you can tell him yourself."

AN INTERNAL DELIVERY van picked us up from outside the space-port and took us into the city. Denni ushered me and Freddi into the back where we sat among some crates labelled as cleaning sup-plies, while she sat up front with the driver.

It gave me a chance to find a copy of the report from my court appearance using my own P-tab. I watched it again and winced when I saw the editing had made my desperation when I shouted 'free Manupia' look more like defiance.

"That's not what happened," said Freddi, when I showed him.

"No," I said.

"They cut out where you said that you didn't do it, that it was a man dressed as a monk and you tried to stop him."

"Yes," I said.

"What are we going to do?"

"See the head of the Free Manupia movement," I said. "I assume that's who this Chrisov is. Or he's a regional commander of some sort. If we can get out of him the identity of the real assassin, then it'll be the first step to clearing my name."

"I can't imagine he's going to be happy to do that," said Freddi. "Your outburst in the court was a gift to them. With all the attention on you, it diverts suspicion away from their own operative."

"Either way, if the Free Manupians ordered the assassination, then they're the ones we're here to see. If Denni takes us straight to see Chrisov, then I can make a personal appeal to him. If he's using my face as propaganda for his cause, then I should have some leverage."

The delivery van dropped us off on a side street somewhere in Shangi city, and Denni led us the rest of the way on foot through deserted, run-down streets to the facade of an abandoned factory. It could have been the same abandoned factory I had been brought to on my original escape from the planet, although I couldn't be sure. I remember it being vast and empty with scant remnants of workstations still welded to the floor and almost pitch black after all the lighting circuits had been stripped out.

The front had two entrances: one big enough for goods vehicles, and a smaller rectangular door suitable for people. Denni hit her fist against the smaller door in a pattern of five knocks and waited.

Moments later, it was opened just enough for the face of a boy, about fifteen years old, to peer out. He was clutching the butt of an EE rifle close to his chest and he deliberately stood so the weapon was clearly visible.

"It's Denni," she said. "I've got two people to see Chrisov."

"Go away, Denni. We've got no time for visitors," said the boy with disdain.

"He'll want to see this one." She stood aside so the boy had a clear view of me.

I smiled politely and his face fell. His superior smirk turned to shock and the red drained from his cheeks. "Stay there," he said.

He went to close the door, but Denni pressed her hand on it to stop him. "I don't think we should wait out here where other people might see us, do you?"

"No," said the boy, all flustered. "Come in."

He backed away and let Denni, then myself and finally Freddi step inside.

I expected to be greeted by the dark surroundings that I had remembered from my previous visit, but – if, indeed, it was the same factory – it had totally changed. Portable lighting units had been brought in and were shining out across the factory floor in several zones where people were gathered. Some of them were sitting on boxes, or possibly delivery crates of some sort, while others were milling around. I couldn't see any of their faces as they were all in shadow and a distance away from the entrance, but I *was* able to see that the boy wasn't the only one with an EE rifle clutched to his body.

The boy ran through the middle of them, shouting: "Chrisov! Chrisov! Chrisov!"

A rumble of disturbance ran through the assembled people, who I took to be Free Manupians, and most of them stood up. Those with weapons didn't aim them, but held them ready to bring into action at any moment.

I waited nervously. Freddi seemed tense as he waited by my side, while Denni just grinned proudly.

The figure of a man, his face in shadow, came striding through the centre of the derelict factory floor towards us. He was flanked by two others who kept a respectful half a pace behind him and posed, as they walked, with one hand on their outer hips so an elbow stuck out on either side. His presence caused a hush to sweep through the building and the beams from the portable lighting units strobed onto his slender body one by one as he passed them.

When he neared us, the ambient light was enough to pick out the features of his face. He was a young man, around the same age as Denni, with large pupils set within light brown eyes, brown hair clipped tightly at the sides but longer on top where it flopped into a fringe. I also saw that the two people on either side of him, both women older than him, were not resting their hands on the bones of their hips, but on personal sidearms which were clipped to their belts.

If these people were the Free Manupians, then they appeared organised and ready for action.

"Chrisov," said Denni, full of enthusiasm. "This is–"

But he was already looking me directly in the eye. I saw the same sense of recognition that I had seen from the people in the bar, along with a subtle smile of satisfaction. "I can see who it is," he said. His voice was soft, smooth and assured. I could see why Denni was so enamoured of him.

"I see my reputation precedes me," I said.

He chuckled at that, revealing the whiteness of his teeth and an easiness that meant he was comfortable in his little hideout surrounded by his armed disciples. "Which makes me surprised that you decided to come back to Manupia after the assassination."

"I need to talk to you about that," I said.

"This can be arranged. But first, I need you to hand over your weapons and P-tabs."

He nodded to his two escorts. One of them held out her hand, palm upwards, to me, while the other did the same to Freddi. Neither of us responded.

"Don't you trust us?" I said.

"It's not that," explained Chrisov. "It's just that we have a policy with new arrivees. I have been very strict with other people and I have always said that I will make no exceptions. Even for you, Sesaan Cassandra."

"I prefer Cassy."

He nodded with respect. "Cassy, then."

The women had not wavered as they waited with their open palms and so, reluctantly, I reached into my pocket for my P-tab and then, even more reluctantly, removed my EEW from its holster. Freddi watched me for a moment, then relented and did the same.

Chrisov turned to the woman who had disarmed me. "Leanna, put those items away safely and see if you can find us some refreshments while Cassy and I talk in private."

"Yes, Chrisov." Leanna retrieved Freddi's items from her fellow escort and disappeared further inside the factory.

Chrisov gestured up ahead and I was about to follow him when the remaining armed woman stepped between me and Freddi and he was forced to stop.

I stopped too. "What about my friend?"

Chrisov looked back and regarded Freddi with curiosity. "He is welcome to refreshments too. Denni, why don't you show him around our humble hideout?"

"But I wanted to–"

"Denni." His voice was cutting. "You want to be useful, don't you?"

"Yes, Chrisov." She smiled, but still looked hurt. She gestured to Freddi. "This way."

But Freddi didn't move. "Cassy?"

I took him aside so we were a couple of metres away from the others and kept my voice low. "Have a look around and see what you can find out while I talk to Chrisov. But if they offer you any coffee, remember not to drink it."

He smiled at the memory of the drugged coffee that made factory workers compliant on Manupia. "You too," he said.

He went with Denni towards one of the gatherings in the makeshift camp while Chrisov led me down the centre of the factory. As I neared the first man sitting on an old packing crate by one of the portable lighting units, he got to his feet. I looked directly into his eyes as I passed and felt a strange sense of admiration from him. At first, I thought it was for Chrisov, but as he continued to watch me, I realised the admiration was aimed in my direction. Others followed his example and began to stand, one after another in a wave of rising people. The young boy who had greeted us at the door with his rifle broke into applause and suddenly twenty people were standing and clapping on either side of us like we were the star attraction in a procession.

I blushed and avoided looking anyone else in the eye as my embarrassment ran deep. What they were applauding was a lie.

I wondered what their reaction would have been if they knew I had actually tried to prevent the assassination from happening.

Chrisov took me to a private area at the side of the factory where four proper chairs had been set out around a circular lighting unit which cast subtle, rather than harsh, light out in 360 degrees. As camps in abandoned factories go, it was relatively comfortable.

Sitting himself on one of the chairs, Chrisov invited me to do the same, as the armed escort kept a respectful distance and stood with her back to us while her hand continued to rest on the EEW at her hip.

"I don't deserve that," I said, referring to the standing ovation I had just been subjected to.

"They think you do," said Chrisov.

"Because of the reports of me in court?"

"Yes," he said.

"Do you know those reports aren't accurate?" I said.

There was no flicker of surprise on his face when he answered. "Yes."

"Then…" I wasn't sure how to phrase the question.

"Then why do I let them believe that they are?" he suggested.

"Yes," I said.

"Because it makes them feel good. You are a hero, Cassy. You single-handedly stopped something that we all feared. That gives them something to believe in."

"Even if it isn't true?"

"There's no need to protest your innocence here, Cassy. You are among friends."

"But I *am* innocent. I didn't fire the shot, it was the monk."

"So you said in court."

His dismissive attitude suddenly angered me. "He was the one who shouted 'free Manupia', not me. He had to be working for you. I need to find out who it was so I can clear my name."

"Why should I tell you that?" said Chrisov. "It's more useful to me that everyone believes you are the assassin. Especially now that you have returned to Manupia."

Leanna, who Chrisov had sent off on a mission to find refreshments, returned carrying a tray containing two bowls of sloppy, brown stew and two cups of steaming hot liquid. I sniffed at the cup she handed to me. It smelled of nothing.

Chrisov laughed at my doubtful expression. "It's perfectly safe to drink."

I peered into the clear, steaming liquid. "What is it?"

"Boiled water," said Chrisov. "We always boil our drinking water."

"You think your water could be contaminated?"

"No, but we know that the coffee they used to give us was. When people join here, we make them go into withdrawal. We've found that giving them hot, plain water gives them some of the sense of drinking coffee without the addictive properties. It has, ironically, become a bit of a habit."

I sipped at it. It did appear to be plain water, as he suggested.

Chrisov chomped down on his stew with large, hungry spoonfuls and encouraged me to do the same.

"So," he said, finishing a mouthful. "It's true that you worked in one of the factories with Denni?"

"Why should I answer your questions when you haven't answered mine?"

187

"The truth is, I don't know the identity of the monk, but I can find out for you if that's what you want."

"That's what I want."

He nodded. "You were going to tell me about Denni."

I sighed and decided it was best to answer in the hope of getting more information out of him. "It's true I worked at the same place as Denni. I was working undercover trying to discover what Prince James wanted with the Manupian factories."

"To close them down and kill all the workers," said Chrisov.

The plain facts, which I had worked so hard to uncover, sounded almost casual coming from his lips. My spoon, which was halfway between carrying some stew from the bowl to my mouth, tipped sideways and deposited its sloppy contents back to where they had come from. "You know about that?"

"It's all in the recordings."

"The recordings?"

"You do not know about the secret recordings?" said Chrisov. "Someone set up surveillance at a meeting between President Udinov and Prince James in which they spoke about their plans. The revelations are shocking to say the least."

I shivered with realisation, and the spoon I was holding fell into the bowl. I remembered strapping a P-tab to a table in the meeting room of the factory and setting it to record shortly before James and Udinov went inside. But I was discovered before I was able to go back and retrieve it. In all the panic of trying to escape, I had forgotten it was even there.

"I see that you didn't know," said Chrisov.

"It's difficult to keep up when you escape from jail and go on the run," I said.

"The recordings are what led to us setting up the Free Manupia movement." Chrisov removed a P-tab from his pocket and played a snippet of an audio file:

"...*the plague will wipe out a large swathe of the population and you will be able to close many of your labour-intensive factories.*" It was James's voice: it sounded woolly and distant from being recorded under a table, but it was unmistakably him. "*You will then be free to install all the automation you want.*"

Another voice, apparently Udinov's, responded: "*I'm concerned about what the population will do. You've already seen the problems we've been having with the workless.*"

"*The plague will be swift.*" James's voice again. "*The population will be so concerned with the illness that civil unrest won't be an issue. Your household and essential personnel will be protected by the vaccine, leaving most of the workers to die out. The few that survive will be enough to carry out any work which can't be achieved through automation. What's more, with them being the last survivors on Manupia, they will be grateful for the work.*"

Chrisov stopped the playback and pocketed the P-tab.

The revelations were, indeed, shocking.

"How did you get the recording?" I said.

"We were lucky," he said. "A cleaner found it by accident. Fortunately, they had the presence of mind to pass it onto the right people."

"Where did the cleaner find it? Was it attached to a table leg at the Jonsonii factory?"

Chrisov looked surprised. "I thought you didn't know about the recordings."

"When I went undercover, I bugged a meeting with James and Udinov using the recording function of my P-tab, but I had to leave it behind."

"Well, Cassy, it seems that we owe you a debt of gratitude that goes beyond the assassination."

"But Udinov was the one behind the plans to release the plague on Manupia. He died. You have President Sophea now. I don't believe she would do such a thing." We had also destroyed the supplies of the plague virus that Udinov and James had conspired to bring to Manupia, not that I had time to explain all that to Chrisov.

"Sophea is still planning to sell us out to the Fertillans."

"How? I thought plans for a political alliance collapsed when the assassin stopped the wedding."

"Not so much stopped as postponed," said Chrisov. "The word is, Sophea is planning another royal wedding."

"But Prince Stephen has been disowned by his own family. What would be the point of Helinea marrying him now?"

"Not Stephen," said Chrisov. "There is another brother."

It took me a moment to realise what he was talking about. "James?"

"And another sister."

"Prince James is going to marry President Sophea?"

"Not if we can stop it," said Chrisov. "That's where you turning up here right now is a lucky break for us, Cassy. You can help us stop a political alliance between Manupia and Fertilla. And, this time, we will stop it for good."

CHAPTER TWENTY THREE

I FOUND FREDDI AT the back of the Free Manupian hideout where the last of the portable light units shone a bright beam across a couple of old packing crates used as chairs. By the look of the empty bowl and cup by his side, Freddi had been given the same food and drink as me. He was alone, as Chrisov had taken the others off to a private meeting, except for a lookout with a rifle who stood at a discreet distance from where the others were gathered.

Freddi came to greet me at the edge of where the beam of light fell away into shadow. "Did they tell you?" he said. "Prince James is going to marry President Sophea."

"So I heard," I said. "What must be going through the woman's mind?"

"I think she's desperate," said Freddi. "From what the people have been telling me, the economic situation on Manupia is getting worse. Factory orders are drying up with competition from other

191

worlds and more people are being made workless. There's been an effort to bring in automation to make the factories more competitive, but that's angered the population. One of the men I was talking to said his job had been replaced by a machine and he's decided to fight for his future. I'm not surprised they've armed themselves and holed up here."

"Sophea thinks marrying James is the solution? When we met her, I thought she had more sense than that."

"According to the official announcement, it will be a glorious union of two planets which will bring much-needed investment into Manupia and herald a bright new future. The people here think it's a way for Fertilla to take control of Manupia without having to resort to conflict."

"Either way, I don't understand why Prince James would be interested in a factory planet in decline."

"Power," said Freddi. "Remember what he said when we saw him with President Udinov before Udinov was killed? It would align the most powerful manufacturing centre in the Obsidian Rim with the major food producer of the region."

"But still… a planet on the verge of civil war with factories which can't compete. It doesn't sound a very enticing proposition to me."

"There are still a lot of resources here," said Freddi. "The best time to acquire resources is when they're cheap. If marrying President Sophea is all it costs, then I imagine Prince James thinks that's a price worth paying. He's probably only annoyed that he can't get his brother to go through with the wedding for him."

A massive cheer rose from where Chrisov had gathered his followers in another part of the factory.

Freddi glanced over at them. "Did you find out anything about the assassin from Chrisov?"

"He won't tell me. He claims not to know who the monk was, but says he will find out."

"Do you believe him?"

I shrugged. "It's difficult to tell."

"If he is going to find out for you, then he needs to do it fast. I don't want to stay here longer than we need to. These people are living on the edge. I got the sense, when they handed me that bowl of stew, that I was stealing food from the mouths of their children."

A round of applause broke out among the people clustered around Chrisov and they began to disperse. From out of the group, Chrisov himself strode tall and confident towards us. He was followed by Leanna who had replaced the subtle EEW at her hip with a more threatening rifle which she held tightly in front of her chest.

"Cassy!" said Chrisov. "I see you've found your friend. He is being well looked after, I trust?"

"I am fine, thank you," said Freddi.

But Chrisov took no notice of Freddi's reply and kept all of his attention on me. "I have discussed it with my team, and we are agreed. You shall appear at the rally we are holding in the centre of Shangi city tomorrow. It will be a great boost to our cause."

I shook my head. "That's not what I'm here for."

"You won't have to say anything, you won't have to do anything. Just appear with me."

"I don't want to get involved in your politics."

"It's a little too late for that, don't you think?" He smiled and waved at the people on the factory floor who had cheered and applauded him only minutes before. Even in the shadows created by the harsh lights of the portable units, I could see they watched us with expectant faces. "Everyone has been told you will do this for us. It wouldn't be nice to let them down."

"Then you should have asked me first."

"Why don't we go over here and discuss it quietly?" He unexpectedly threw an arm around my waist. Outwardly it would look like a friendly gesture, but the way he grabbed me felt like exactly the opposite.

He propelled me a couple of steps forward and Freddi tried to follow, but Leanna stepped in his way and held her rifle like some kind of barrier.

"Cassy, are you okay?" Freddi called out from behind her.

I pushed Chrisov away from my body, but he pulled me back tighter and that's when I felt the sharp point of a knife in my side. I tensed and stopped struggling, since the blade was pressing through the thin membrane of my shirt. "Tell your friend everything is fine," Chrisov whispered in my ear.

"It's okay, Freddi, I'll be back in a minute."

Chrisov led me further into the darkness and I saw Freddi's worried face watching us from behind Leanna's rifle.

"You wouldn't stab me," I said to Chrisov. "I'm supposed to be your hero."

"It's true you're worth more to me alive," he said. "But if you have to become a martyr to our cause, then I could arrange it. There has been talk of someone from Manupian security trying to infiltrate our group – it would be awful if we found out who it was and you accidentally got shot as they tried to escape. Or perhaps you would survive while your friend over there got killed."

194

I glanced back at where Freddi was pacing behind Leanna, limping a little as his hip was playing up with the stress. He appeared so vulnerable, like an animal in a cage, and I knew that with the knife in my side, I was in no position to help him.

"Freddi has nothing to do with this."

"And I can keep him out of it, if you agree to appear at the rally tomorrow. I will even tell you about the monk, if that would make you feel better."

"You will give me his name?" I said.

"I will tell you what I know," said Chrisov.

"Okay, fine," I said. They already had my image shouting 'free Manupia' in the courtroom. Anything else I did couldn't make it any worse. "I will appear at your rally if that's what it takes."

Chrisov's face broke out into a broad smile. He slipped the knife back into the inside of his jacket and withdrew his arm from around my waist. "Excellent!" he declared in a booming voice so everyone could hear. "Then it is all arranged."

Chapter Twenty Four

THEY SAID THEY weren't guarding us, but they were guarding us.

There were people on duty with rifles ostensibly keeping an eye on the camp, but any time we moved it felt as if they were keeping an eye on us. Freddi and I could get up from our seats and walk around freely, but on the one occasion we approached the exit, the person on guard there was very sure to stand in the way of the door and to keep their rifle in sight. I was told that security considerations meant it was too dangerous to venture out at that time of night, although I got the impression that if we tried to leave in the morning, it would be the same story.

Through all of this, I was worried about Stephen. It was a long time since we had sent him back to the shuttle to wait for us. I asked Chrisov about contacting him using my P-tab, but those same 'security considerations' that stopped us leaving, also banned the use of P-tabs. At least, for us. The other people hiding out in the abandoned factory didn't seem to be under the same restriction. Freddi offered to try to pickpocket a P-tab from someone and, although I didn't doubt that he could do it, the risk of getting caught was greater than my concern over contacting Stephen. If Stephen had any sense – and I hoped to the Deity he had – he would hold tight until he heard something from us.

In the morning, the Free Manupians packed up around us and prepared for the rally. There was to be a procession through the streets of Shangi to culminate in some sort of mass gathering in the centre where I would be presented to the crowd. Chrisov, all pleasant and polite, explained that there was no room for Freddi in the lead party and he would be better off joining with the marchers in the procession. By the way it was explained to me, I got the impression that Freddi would be kept under guard separately as some sort of insurance policy to make sure I did not renege on my side of the agreement.

I promised Freddi I would meet him back at the shuttle after the rally and I hoped he could tell, from my worried expression, that it meant he should try to get away from the others as soon as possible. We wished each other luck and, as he left the factory with an armed man at his side, I knew that's exactly what he was going to do.

Denni left shortly afterwards with another group of people and stopped off briefly to say goodbye. She didn't seem fazed at all by the fact she seemed to be part of a paramilitary organisation and I wasn't sure if it was because she believed passionately in the cause, or was secretly in love with Chrisov. Either way, I suspected it would be the last time I would see her.

A small delivery van, very much like the one that had brought us to Chrisov's hideout – if not the same one – came in via the goods vehicle entrance and was loaded up with several boxes, some of which appeared to be freestanding speakers. I was then asked to sit in the back, along with Leanna and her rifle. She sat with it resting on her lap – guarding me while appearing not to be guarding me – and then Chrisov clambered aboard and took up a position between us. The other person to join us in the back of the van was the boy who had opened the door when we arrived. He also had a rifle and cradled it like it was some kind of valued pet.

I kept a mental note of the number of streets we went down and the corners that we turned while we travelled inside the van. From my memory of visiting Shangi before, and from my understanding of where the abandoned factory was, it felt like we were heading directly into the centre of the city. Chrisov stared straight ahead during the whole journey, as if in personal contemplation, and no one else dared say a word.

The van let us out on a side street of terraced houses that extended away from us in a uniform pattern of repeating front doors and windows. At the bottom of the street was the mass of movement and colour of marchers advancing on our position. The sound of their footsteps beat hard on the ground, while their indecipherable chanting echoed up the street with a melodic resonance.

A group of Free Manupians, with neck scarves pulled up over their noses to disguise their faces, were waiting for us. They unloaded the equipment from the van and took it off in the opposite direction to the marchers. It was only when the van pulled away that I saw we were close to the end of the street where it opened up into a large space. Leanna and the boy tied scarves around their faces like the others and flanked Chrisov and myself while we headed towards it.

The vast space was actually an open square created by four buildings which faced into the middle. All of them had the same white-painted facade and rows upon rows of windows that looked out onto a statue reaching up to the artificial sky at the centre of the square. The statue was of a young man who looked very much like some of the factory workers I had worked with on my previous visit to Manupia. Cast from a silvery grey metal, he had an impressive, lithe figure which was dressed in dungaree-style overalls. On one hand, he wore a protective industrial glove and, in the other, he held a large hammer up above his head like a trophy raised in celebration. He stood upon a raised plinth which was as tall as me and reachable only by climbing a set of three large steps cut into the base.

The people with their scarves over their faces were already clambering over the plinth and setting up speakers on each corner. Watching them from in front of the buildings were the black-clad figures of Manupian security. Each was armed with an EE rifle, but there were only two of them per building, which meant there were only eight in total. That was almost a match for the number of armed Free Manupians who were already there, and with many more yet to arrive, they would certainly be outnumbered.

The sound of the marchers was getting closer. Not just from behind us, but also from the three other streets that funnelled into the square. The groundswell of so many people converging on one place was both magical and frightening. Their collective voices seemed so powerful that they were greater than a blast from an EEW and stronger than the authority of a ruling president.

Leanna grabbed my hand. "This way," she said and she ran to the statue as the first of the marchers began to filter into the square. We went up the steps to where some packing crates had been stacked to form some kind of barrier and we sat down behind them with our bottoms on the cold, hard surface of the plinth and our backs to the majestic statue of the factory worker.

"We stay here until Chrisov is ready for you," she said.

"When's that?" I asked.

"You'll know when."

My view of the square was obscured by the crates, but I could hear the excited voices of more and more marchers entering into the space. Within minutes, the individual voices had merged to become a single mass of noise.

Against the mishmash of voices, the lyrical melody of a song drifted through. At first, it was just a few people singing, but as more joined it became an empowering anthem. *"Free Manupia,"* they sang. Two simple words repeated over and over along a rising and falling scale of five basic notes.

I looked around and saw that, as well as Leanna sitting next to me with her rifle, there were at least four others standing guard on the plinth with rifles or smaller EE weapons.

The song flittered away as I heard Chrisov's voice boom over the speakers set up around us.

"Manupians, welcome!" he declared.

Cheering filled the square.

"It is gratifying to see so many of you out here today to claim the right to have your say in your own destiny."

They cheered again.

"For the workless among you, I know how hard your struggle has been over these recent months and years. For those of you who are employed, I feel the dread you have every day when you walk to the factory and fear that it might be your last. We are here to tell you, President Sophea, that the job losses must stop! The factory closures must stop! The people must be listened to!"

The last of his words were almost drowned out by enthusiastic applause.

"She tells you that an alliance with Fertilla will solve our problems. But you, my friends, have heard the recordings. You know what the Fertillans would like to do to us – kill us and replace us with machines! But we say 'no'! We will not be conquered by another planet. We will continue to live and manufacture products that are the envy of the Obsidian Rim and we will be free! Free Manupia!"

"Free Manupia! Free Manupia! Free Manupia!"

"So we will stop this sham of a wedding with the royal Fertillan prince," he called out over the chanting, which subsided at the sound of his voice. "We will prevent a political alliance from bringing death to this planet. We've done it before and we will do it again – and I have the proof!"

Leanna grabbed me by the elbow and pulled me to my feet. "You're on," she said in my ear.

Chrisov appeared from behind one of the speakers and took my hand. He tried to pull me forward, but I resisted. "Tell me about the monk first," I said.

He glanced back at the crowd who were cheering and clapping in anticipation. "After your appearance," he said.

"Now!" I demanded. "Or I won't do it."

His eyes narrowed with anger and impatience and he nodded to Leanna to withdraw. She stepped back dutifully and he pulled my hand to bring me closer to him. "The truth is, I don't know who the monk was," he said into my ear so the others couldn't hear. "I didn't send him and the leaders in the other cities didn't either – if they had, they wouldn't hesitate to claim responsibility. We couldn't have smuggled an assassin and their weapon into such a heavily guarded building on another planet even if we wanted to. We're grateful that he shouted 'free Manupia', but he wasn't one of our operatives. We think it was a rouse to throw you – or anyone else who heard him – off the scent."

As he drew back from me, I looked into his face and I saw no reason to believe he was lying. The revelation took all the wind out of me and I stood there dumbfounded, trying to understand how I could have been duped by two simple words.

"Now, you need to fulfil your side of the bargain," said Chrisov. "Or would you like me to send word to the people who are guarding your friend?"

His hand still holding tight onto mine, he yanked me forward and I stumbled out from behind the speakers to find myself looking out onto a vast crowd, not only packed into the square, but also extending out into the four streets that fed into it. Gasps rose up from some of those at the front as they were close enough to see my face. The murmured word *assassin, assassin, assassin* broke out in several places in the rows closest to me and spread further and further back like the hissing of hundreds of snakes.

The sight of so many people staring at me, many of them with eyes peering over the scarves that covered their faces, was so intimidating that I could almost feel their eyes penetrating me.

I searched what I could see of their red, angry faces – spurred on by Chrisov's rousing words – in the hope of seeing Freddi among them. Freddi wasn't there and I hoped he had managed to escape already. But there was one pair of blue eyes, peering out over the top of a scarf three rows back from the front, that drew me in. They were Stephen's eyes, watching me intently from beneath the fringe of his brown hair tipped with yellowish blonde. As I stared back, he put a finger to where his lips were underneath his scarf and I forced myself to turn away and pretend I had seen nothing.

Chrisov raised my hand up above our heads in a victory salute like the statue of the man behind us held his hammer. "Here is the assassin who killed the Fertillan Queen to save us!" The roar of cheers and applause from the enthusiastic crowd intensified.

Chrisov turned, forcing me to turn as well, to show my face to each of the four sides of the crowded square. "Here is the proof that we will not be dictated to! Here is the proof that we will not let another planet take our lives away from us! Here is the proof that we will not rest until Manupia is free!"

The adulation all around us turned, in an instant, to shock, as Chrisov spun away from me as if someone had knocked him in the shoulder. His hand was wrenched from mine and he was sent flying onto his back. He landed hard on the plinth beneath the statue and reached up to clasp his shoulder where there was the red mess of a bleeding EE wound. Screams erupted all around me as the crowd in the front rows realised what was going on.

Leanna jumped to my side and pulled at my arm. "Get down!"

I did as I was told as another EE blast ripped through the air where my head had been and singed the statue's knee. Half crouching, half running, we made it to the edge of the plinth just as a metal ball landed next to us and began bellowing smoke. Leanna let go of me to put two hands on her rifle and swing round in the direction of whoever threw it.

My next breath took in a mouthful of smoke and it stung my throat like acid. My eyes filled with tears and my vision went blurry. The more I blinked, the more I worked the smoke into my eyes. I lost track of where Leanna had gone. The more I kept my eyes open, the more the smoke brushed at my eyeballs and caused the tear ducts to produce moisture to try to wash the pain away.

Someone was at the microphone and yelling through the speakers. It was a man's voice, but not Chrisov's. "Everyone stay calm and no one will get hurt! Raise your hands and walk slowly and carefully out of the square."

By the sounds of the screams and cries of panic, no one was doing anything slowly and carefully.

Unseen hands grabbed at my shoulders and I twisted to break free from them.

"Cassy, Cassy, it's me!" It was Stephen's voice.

"Stephen?" I turned to him, but all I saw was the blurred outline of his face partly covered by a scarf before the pain in my eyes forced me to close them shut.

"Come on, let's get you out of here," he said.

He propelled me to the edge of the plinth. The smoke wasn't so thick there and I stopped to take in deep breaths.

Stephen took my hand and placed something damp into my palm. "Breathe through this, it will help filter out the gas."

"But my eyes are stinging. I can barely see."

"I know. I'll help you."

I put the damp cloth to my face and allowed Stephen to take my arm and help me slowly down the steps to the ground level of the square. In front of us, I could see the outlines of people running in all directions. Some of them were clutching the unmistakable shapes of rifles. I almost tripped over three people lying on the floor who had become tangled and incapacitated in the blue mesh of a riot net. Two of them lay still, but the third one was thrashing around, causing the electricity in its cables to jolt them with painful sparks.

"Stephen, what's going on?"

"Manupian security just over-stepped their remit," he said.

A shadow passed across my face and another canister hit the ground to the side of us. Stephen abruptly changed direction and pushed me away from the billowing cloud of gas. We hurried through the middle of the square towards one of the streets where a crush of people were trying to get out. But, before we got there, the blur of something blue streaked across my vision. Stephen must have seen it too because he yanked me back, but not before the riot net came down on top of us. Shocks fired through my body and I collapsed to the ground with electricity stabbing all over me. I tried to free myself from the tangle but, with each movement, it shocked me again and encased me tighter in its web.

CHAPTER TWENTY FIVE

WITH ALL THAT I had been through in feigning death to escape Fertilla, travelling beyond the edge of the galaxy and finding the people behind the Free Manupia movement, it seemed that my only achievement was to swap a Fertillan jail cell for a Manupian one.

There was very little difference between the two rooms. The Manupian cell was not carved out of the planet's crust like the Fertillan one, but it was just as small and just as locked. Its only features were a hard bench for me to sit on and a door without a handle on the inside for me to stare at. Which I did for many hours.

Stephen and I had got separated soon after being caught in the riot net. I saw him being led away in the other direction as I was bundled into the back of a Manupian security van and no matter how much I screamed or begged, no one would tell me where they were taking him or what was going to happen to me. My body still ached from the after-effects of the net and I could feel the bruises on my arms and legs where its cables had shocked me into submission. My eyes were sore from the gas, but my vision had returned. My throat was scratchy, although I was able to breathe normally, even if it still hurt a little bit and I yearned for some water. Nobody came to bring me water, nobody came to question me or tell me my rights. It was like they had thrown me in there and forgotten about me.

Eventually, the sound of locks releasing on the cell door caused me to start out of my stupor. I sat up straight on the bench, ready to face my jailer.

In my head, I rehearsed all the demands I was going to make and all the legal rights that I could remember were afforded to a Fertillan citizen on another world.

But my appeals died on my lips as the last person I expected to see walked through the door. "Stephen?"

He had buzzed his hair free of the yellowish blonde dye, he was clean-shaven, washed, and his clothes were uncrumpled. Like he had never been out on the streets and caught in a riot net at all.

"Cassy, I've found you at last!"

I stood up to greet him as he came forward and encased me in a strong hug. The joy of seeing him made me want to sink into his embrace and bury myself away in it for a long time. But I had too many questions.

"What happened?" I said, as I pulled myself back.

"Manupian security is in chaos," he said. "They took no records, they don't know who they arrested or where they put them. I had to check each cell…"

"No, stop!" I sat myself down on the bench and leant back against the cold cell wall. "Start at the beginning. How did you know I would be at the rally? What were you doing there? How come they let you go?"

"When you didn't come back from the bar, I decided to find Helinea."

"The woman you were going to marry?"

Stephen nodded and came to sit next to me on the bench. "She knew I wasn't involved in the assassination. In fact, a few steps to one side and that EE blast could have hit me. I ran away with you, obviously, so there was a chance she would have me arrested and extradited back to Fertilla, but on the few occasions we had met, I understood her to be a reasonable woman."

"So, you just turned up at her house and knocked on the door?"

He chuckled. "Something like that, yes. I went to Manupian Headquarters. It seems that being a Fertillan prince, even a disgraced one, is enough for people to open doors for you."

"I still don't understand what you were doing at the rally."

"Helinea was able to share with me some intelligence from a spy embedded in the Free Manupia movement that you were going to appear at a mass demonstration in the centre of the city."

"I didn't want to do it, Stephen, but I had no choice."

"I know," he said. "I could see it in your eyes when you were dragged in front of the crowd. Helinea also told me the security services were going to use the rally as an opportunity to take the Free Manupia leader into custody, and I wanted to try to pull you out before there was any trouble. But someone in the crowd got trigger happy, riot protocol was enabled and the whole thing was carnage. Getting caught up in that net and being locked up in here was probably the safest thing that could have happened to you."

"What about Freddi? Do you know if he's okay? We got separated."

"He's fine. He was able to slip away from the rally and make it to the shuttle. He's worried about you, though."

I took a deep breath, leant back against the cell wall and pressed its coolness onto my skull as I let the last of my tension slip away. "So, what happens now?"

"I'll contact Helinea and see if she can get you released," said Stephen. "But she'll need to appeal directly to her sister, the president, and that might be more difficult. After that, I'm not sure. Did you get anywhere in finding out who the assassin was?"

"Chrisov claimed the monk was nothing to do him or any of the leaders in the other cities."

"Do you believe him?"

I shrugged. "He's a very charismatic man and I'm sure he's a good liar. But, yeah, I believe him. He said shouting 'free Manupia' was a way to throw me off the scent and I think he was probably right. It seems that we may have been looking for the assassin on the wrong planet."

Chapter Twenty Six

I WAS TAKEN FROM my cell in handcuffs and bundled into the back of a Manupian security van just like the one which had carried me away from the rally. I thought I would see Stephen waiting for me, but he was not there. My ankles were shackled to restraints inside the van so I had no way of escape and I feared that the optimism Stephen had given me was merely false hope.

After a short drive, I was transferred to an airtight personnel carrier which had the capacity to travel on the surface of the planet. It reminded me of the car I had first taken to Manupian Headquarters, which is separate from the cities in its own environmental enclosure, back when I was working undercover as a spy on Prince James's ship. I took my chance to turn my head sideways and see through the front windscreen of the vehicle to catch a glimpse of the exterior of the dusty, yellow planet with the grey mound of the HQ in the distance.

The security official barked at me to look straight ahead and I did as I was told. I had seen enough to realise where I was being taken.

Once inside the building and the airlock had closed behind us, I was pulled out of the car and marched by two security officials through the wide, opulent hallways of the planet's headquarters. I remembered the way from previous visits, but was surprised to be taken to the double doors which I remembered being the entrance to a grand sitting room for the president, their family and their guests. The room had been sealed off when I was last there while a fire was allowed to rage inside and destroy any trace of the plague virus which had been used to kill President Udinov, Sophea's father.

One of the officials knocked on the right-hand door, a female voice behind it ordered us to enter, and we obeyed.

It was as if there had never been a fire at all. The spacious room with its high ceiling was decorated in a pristine, smooth white surface with drapes of finely embroidered material hanging from the back wall to deaden the echo inside and give the room a sense of grandeur. Under my feet was the spongey feel of a new carpet in a deep red colour that was patterned with yellow diamond shapes, upon which sat four tall-backed armchairs covered in plush golden-yellow velvet. Stephen, who was sitting in one of them, got to his feet as I entered. In another one of the chairs sat a woman I recognised as Helinea. She had tied back her long curls of light brown hair so they were away from her face and she wore a plain, light green shift dress that flowed down to her calves with a lightweight cardigan on top which matched the colour of her hair. She did not look as stunning as she had on her wedding day, but her natural beauty was enough to shine out from her simple choice of clothing.

Half of the room was taken up by a large desk made of what looked like real wood with a screen rising out of the middle of it. Behind it sat President Sophea.

She had let her natural blonde hair drape across her shoulders where it rested on the top of a long sleeveless maroon robe which she wore over a more formal black trouser suit. I remembered Sophea as being an attractive young woman, but she seemed to have aged in the year since I had seen her. The strain of running a planet in decline was beginning to show in the lines forming on her face.

She stood and gestured impatiently at the two security guards who had brought me. "Leave us!"

The officials departed my side, stepped out of the room and I heard the double doors close behind me. I stood, somewhat nervously, with my hands still cuffed in front of me.

"Surely those are not necessary, Lady President," said Stephen, indicating the cuffs that bound my wrists.

"With all the trouble she's caused me, she can stay like that as far as I'm concerned," said Sophea as she came out from behind her desk and stood in front of the armchairs to stare into my face.

Her stare was harsh and intimidating. "I'm sorry, it wasn't my intention to cause trouble," I said.

"Not your intention?" she scoffed. "I would hate to see the outcome when it *is* your intention! Do you realise what damage your little outburst in the courtroom has done? I'm trying to save the population of Manupia and all they're doing is turning against me. The only reason the factories are kept going at all is because I'm selling our goods at a loss. We're trying to bring in automation slowly to make the factories more competitive. If we succeed, then we can build more factories and Manupia will be strong again, but I'm running out of places that will lend me money to do it. I had a deal with the Fertillan royal family, a *good* deal until my sister's wedding was called off because of the assassination."

"I tried to stop it," I said. "It's like I said in the court – which you can hear if you watch the full, undoctored footage – I found the monk by accident. When I saw what he was going to do, I tried get the rifle away from him, but he managed to fire off a shot. I'm sorry it killed Queen Triana and her unborn baby, but if I hadn't been there, he might have shot you or Helinea."

I looked across at Helinea, the only one still sitting calmly in her seat and watching me with curiosity. "We were talking about that before you arrived," she said. "Stephen has been developing a theory that the assassin didn't miss. He thinks the assassin might have killed his intended target, don't you, Stephen?"

"Yes." He looked across at Sophea for permission. "If you'll allow me, Lady President."

She waved a dismissive hand as if she didn't care if he continued.

"I was thinking, how could the Free Manupia movement manage to get an operative, and a weapon, into the Halls of the Deity when everyone there had been triple checked and the building was the most tightly guarded in the system, if not the galaxy? As head of the Fertillan Guard, I oversaw the whole of the security arrangements for the wedding, so I know how good they were. At first, I thought I had missed something, that I had been lax in some way because of my own..." He glanced across at Helinea, who acknowledged his look with a smile. "My own nervousness at the approaching ceremony. Any security measure can be countermanded, after all, if your opponent is clever enough. Which made me question what opponent would be capable of doing such a thing and would have the motive to carry it out? The Free Manupians, despite their fervour, are mostly desperate ex-factory workers tied to this planet. Why would they wait until Sophea or Helinea had left the planet to try to assassinate them? It doesn't make sense. Then I wondered if they had been the assassin's target at all – you said, Cassy, that you tried to stop the monk and he may have not had the chance to aim accurately. But maybe he was a better marksman than that. Maybe he intended to shoot Queen Triana all along. So I asked myself, who would benefit from the death of Queen Triana and her unborn child?"

He left the suggestion hanging in the air and the pieces of the jigsaw puzzle fell into place in my mind. "Prince James," I said.

"James has always resented that it was our brother, Richard, who was made King when our father died," said Stephen. "Because he's Richard's twin, he saw himself as his equal until the fact that he came out of the womb second denied him the throne. As next in line, he always had the possibility that the position might become his one day. But Richard marrying Triana changed all that and, with the birth of their first child, James would no longer be next in line. Not only would Queen Triana's son become heir, any more children she had would move James even further down the line of succession until the chances of him gaining power by right of royal birth were close to impossible."

"Interesting," said President Sophea, leaning an elbow on the back of one of the unoccupied armchairs. "But can you prove it?"

Stephen took a deep breath. "Not yet."

"Then your theory is nothing more than gossip and speculation," she said.

"But if I could get back to Fertilla and question my guards, I could uncover the truth."

"You're a fugitive from your own regime!" Sophea declared. "You can no more go back to Fertilla than I can walk out of this building and breathe the air on the planet's surface."

"But, Lady President, you cannot go ahead and marry James knowing what he has done."

"Don't presume to come into my home and tell me what I can and cannot do!" She stood up straight again and her face went red with anger. "If you're telling me that I cannot marry Prince James because he is a little shit, then that's old news. I was here – *here*, remember – when James revealed he had schemed with my father to poison the planet and modernise the factories over the dead bodies of Manupian workers. I *know* what the man is. It gives me no pleasure, I can assure you, to think of sharing his bed once we are married. But he has me cornered, and he knows it. This information you brought me is useful, as it gives me ammunition to use against him while I assert my authority in the relationship. But, if you think you are going to use me as a method of going back home to your little princely comforts, then you can forget it. I saw the deal between us and Fertilla collapse after the disaster of the first wedding, I will not let another wedding fail and see Manupia ruined."

Her voice stopped, but her anger still filled the room.

A knock on the double doors broke the silence and we all turned to see a woman in Manupian security uniform enter.

"What now?!" demanded Sophea, and the official virtually jumped out of her uniform.

"Excuse me, Lady President, but you asked to be informed when Chief Inspector Polinov was here."

"Here's another man who thinks it's a better idea to cause trouble than to do what I say." Sophea sighed with irritation, as if letting out her frustration to the rest of us was going to help. "I told him to bring Chrisov in for questioning *quietly* after the rally. Not shoot him and send in the riot squad."

The security official cowered uncertainly by the door. "I told him to wait, Lady President, but I can tell him to leave if you want."

"No, I'll talk to the drakh-face," she said, striding across the carpet. "He's lucky nobody was killed, or 'talk' is not the only thing I would do to him."

The official jumped out of Sophea's way as she barged through the door and out into the corridor.

Stephen looked worried. "But Lady President!" He charged after her. "Sophea!"

Helinea also got up to follow them and I was left in the ostentatious room on my own. With no one to stop me, I went over to one of the golden high-backed chairs and sat down. The cushion softened under my bottom just enough to be comfortable, but not too much that I sank into it. I looked down at my cuffed hands in my lap and felt how the metal was cutting into my wrists after being encased in them for so long.

It was a metaphor for my situation. I was out of the cell, but not out of trouble. Stephen had clearly believed that bringing the revelation about James to President Sophea's ear would help him win her support. But she was right, it was only a theory and none of us had the power to challenge James without proof.

The door opened again and I thought it would be Stephen returning after his fruitless attempt trying to talk to Sophea. But it was actually Helinea. I stood up, conscious that I had sat in the chair without any invitation.

216

"I'm not the president, you don't need to stand on my account," said Helinea as she approached.

She smiled as I sat and, to my surprise, she crouched down in front of me. In her hand, she held a flat, oval fob which I recognised as the device for operating the handcuffs. She typed out a code on the buttons on its surface and the metal encasing my wrists clicked open and fell into my lap. Helinea tossed the cuffs across the room and they landed underneath Sophea's desk.

"Thank you," I said, and rubbed the circulation back into my sore wrists.

"My sister sometimes forgets how to treat guests," she said.

"She seems to be under a lot of strain."

"Yes," said Helinea. She stood from her crouching position and went back to sit in her chair. "You know, Stephen still holds a torch for you."

"A torch?"

"A man doesn't throw away his position to break someone out of jail if he has no feelings for them. I'm curious what the two of you plan to do now."

I shrugged. "I don't know. I thought I could come to Manupia and clear my name, but that doesn't seem possible."

"I meant the two of you. You know, as a couple."

"Oh." I blushed. "That's complicated."

"Is it? It doesn't seem so to me. It's not as if Stephen is still going to marry me."

"I'm genuinely sorry about that. I never meant to get in the way of the two of you."

"Don't be sorry." Helinea looked away from me and a sadness came over her. "Since I was a little girl, I had an image of

217

what my wedding day would be like. I imagined it would be some fairytale romance and I would be the beautiful princess who everyone would admire. Then I got older and realised that marrying a prince has nothing to do with romance, it is all to do with politics and alliances and money. I still got to dress like a beautiful princess on the day, but then I was splattered with the blood of a murdered pregnant woman who collapsed and died in front of me and the fairytale was over."

"It must have been awful," I said.

"It was. Especially for Queen Triana and King Richard." Tears of the memory formed in her eyes, but she sniffed and forced them away with a reflective smile. "But, in some ways, I'm glad I don't have to carry the burden of the political alliance that my marriage was supposed to create. That's fallen to my sister now and she tells me she has the strength to bear it. Although, sometimes I wonder if she is telling me the truth."

Stephen came back into the room. He looked annoyed and frustrated. "Sophea won't help us," he said. "She thinks marrying James is her last chance to save Manupia and she might be right."

Helinea stood and walked over to the double doors which Stephen had left open to the corridor. She closed them quietly and turned to face us. "That doesn't mean that I can't help you," she said.

Stephen shook his head. "Helinea, I can't ask you to do that."

"You're not asking, I'm offering," she said. "Tell me again about Eden and the new food that could feed the Obsidian Rim."

"I can do better than that," said Stephen. "I can show you."

CHAPTER TWENTY SEVEN

T HE GREEN OF Eden's hemispheres filled the screen on
President Sophea's desk and Helinea watched with open-
mouthed astonishment. The footage which Stephen had taken on
his P-tab was rough and a little bit shaky in places, but it showed
the splendour of the four environments where the hybrid plants
thrived. From the cold of a world without a breathable atmosphere,
to the heat of a colony where sunlight was fierce, to the desert of
a world in perpetual drought, to the harsh conditions of an airless
planet where the freezing temperatures of the night gave way to
the scorching temperatures of the day.

The images ran out, the picture abruptly cut and the screen
turned to black.

Helinea picked up Stephen's P-tab which had been broadcast-
ing the images to her sister's computer and swivelled round on her
chair to look at me and Stephen standing behind her. "We could
grow this food on Manupia?" she asked.

"I'm not a scientist," said Stephen. "But I don't see why not."

"Manupia is one of the easier planets," I said. "There's air, even if it isn't breathable and, although it's a cold, dry planet, the temperatures aren't as extreme as many of the colonies on the Rim."

"It could make us self-sufficient," she said.

"More than that," said Stephen. "Manupia could be the springboard for exporting the new food technology to the rest of the Rim. Propagating the plants so they can be grown on other colonies is a labour-intensive job. Fertilla couldn't spare the labour, but Manupia has people crying out for work."

"Factory workers who know nothing about farms," said Helinea.

"They don't need to know," said Stephen. "Fertilla has the farming expertise to oversee the project, while it's unskilled labour that you can provide. Much of the scientific work still needs to be done, but the hemispheres on Eden prove it's possible. Only, James would never agree to it. In his eyes, Fertilla's wealth comes from its agriculture and he's scared of any technology which he thinks might threaten that."

"But you are not?" she suggested.

"I think Fertilla is more resilient. If it's possible for most of the Rim to feed itself, then we shouldn't stand in its way. Fertillan farmers and scientists can be at the forefront of developing the technology from what we found on Eden. Eventually, Fertilla could focus on more specialist food, like pure SolPrime crops that can't be grown anywhere apart from our agro-domes, or luxury items like coffee or fruit."

Helinea tapped Stephen's P-tab on her chin in thought. "If Sophea marries James and the alliance goes ahead as planned, none of this will happen."

"But you said you could help us," I said.

"I can take you in my wedding party. I'm following on after Sophea in a separate ship and you could pose as members of my crew. With my diplomatic immunity, you will bypass the usual checks on arrival and I could probably get you into the wedding venue."

"That would be amazing," I said.

"Yes, thank you, Helinea," said Stephen.

"Don't thank me yet. That won't be enough to clear Cassy's name and let you back into the royal household. The planet believes Cassy is guilty and you are her foolish, treacherous lover. Your Fertillan Guard may have been loyal to you once, but how many could you trust since they have switched allegiances? How many could you question before one of them turns you in? I'm willing to bet, not many."

Once again, the hope that I had been given felt like it had been ripped from me, torn to pieces and discarded on the carpet. I glanced across at Stephen whose face had turned almost the same colour as the yellow velvet armchairs on the other side of the ostentatious room.

"What you need is irrefutable proof," said Helinea and swivelled back round to face the screen.

"Computer!" she ordered. "Show me the broadcast footage of the marriage of Helinea of Manupia to Prince Stephen of Fertilla." She quickly glanced back to Stephen. "I know that we have it because I caught one of my staff watching it last week – I was so angry, I nearly took her head off."

The computer's unemotional, female voice responded. "There is only footage of the abandoned ceremony."

221

"Well, obviously that's what I meant!" Helinea let out an irritated sigh and calmed herself. "Please play the footage of the abandoned ceremony, computer."

The image of the crowd packed into the Halls of the Deity filled the screen and the harmonious sound of a string quartet played from the speakers. I had a horrible feeling of déjà vu and the sense that I was about to re-watch something traumatic. But, on the screen in front of us, none of the people were aware of that and close-ups of King Richard, Queen Triana, Prince James and President Sophea coming onto the stage showed their happy, smiling faces.

"The whole thing was recorded. Of course!" said Stephen, leaning closer into the screen.

"But surely they couldn't have recorded the assassin," I said. "Or no one could have ever claimed it was me."

"Watch!" said Helinea. "See how the image cuts between different views of the main hall. It's so common in the things we watch that we don't even notice it. I only thought about it when I caught someone else watching it in the Headquarters because I saw what I looked like in my wedding dress from both the front and the back. That is, before I screamed at her to turn it off and sent her running to the kitchen."

Helinea was right. I watched the footage change from a close-up of the Supreme Monk to a wide shot of the expectant crowd, a medium shot of Stephen and Helinea walking up the aisle and then a pan around the sides of the hall to the wealthy people who watched from boxes on the higher level. I saw the same portly grey-bearded gentleman, bejewelled woman and their children who I had seen upstairs in the Halls of the Deity as they leant out from their box to get a better look at the ceremony. The camera panned around further and, to my astonishment, I saw myself.

"That's me!" I pointed at the screen.

It was only for a moment, the image was not close, but it was enough to see my blue dress and the braid of my hair resting across my collarbone before the image changed again.

Helinea stood from her seat. "I'm not going to watch any more, if you don't mind."

She stepped out from behind the desk and walked across to the other side of the room as the footage continued to play. The wedding guests stood to sing the Fertillan anthem and I saw that Stephen's expression had turned into a fixed stare as he continued to watch. There was a close-up of King Richard singing with gusto, a glimpse of the portly gentleman and the bejewelled lady standing in the box and back to a wide shot of the guests in the main hall with Stephen and Helinea standing in front of the Supreme Monk.

Without warning, the streak of an EEW blast shot across the screen. Queen Triana collapsed to the floor and the screen went blank. The singing abruptly ceased and left an eerie silence in the room.

Stephen leant forward on the back of the empty chair that Helinea had been sitting in as he continued to stare at where the images had been moments before. Helinea clasped her hands in front of her and looked down at her thumbs which she had intertwined around each other so tightly that her skin was almost white.

The memories the footage evoked in me were quite different, but I had tried to ignore them to watch for evidence of the assassin. Evidence that was not there. "But you can't see anything!" I said.

"The only thing this footage proves is that I was there in the box with a clear view to shoot the Queen."

"The broadcast version, yes." Helinea nodded. "My understanding is, it was broadcast live to Fertilla, but obviously with the interstellar distances, it couldn't be transmitted to Manupia and we were due to get an edited version. Which, obviously, never happened."

"I don't follow," I said. "If the footage proves nothing, then what use is it to us?"

"*That* footage doesn't," she said. "But what about the footage that was never broadcast? There were cameras in the Halls of the Deity covering multiple angles of the ceremony including, as you pointed out, the boxes. If they were recorded to be put together into a more considered edited version at a later date, then it could be that your monk with the rifle appears on one of them."

Stephen allowed more of his weight to rest on the back of the chair as her words sunk in. "Irrefutable proof," he said under his breath.

"Then, if those recordings still exist, they must be on Fertilla," I said.

Helinea nodded. "As I said, I can take you there, but once we reach the Halls of the Deity, you're on your own."

Chapter Twenty Eight

HELINEA TOOK US on board her ship and gave her crew strict orders not to remark on our presence to anyone inside or outside of her closed circle. She supplied us with the standard black uniforms of Manupian security officials and, from the point of view of any outside observer, we became part of the crew. In truth, we took no part in running the ship and made an effort to keep ourselves out of everyone else's way for the journey.

Before we left for Fertilla, I was briefly able to exchange messages with Freddi. He offered to come with us, but he had already risked himself too much for a fight that wasn't his and I insisted he go back to the ship. In any case, Helinea had said she would smuggle only the two of us to Fertilla and she had no room for a third. Freddi agreed to wait and I made him promise that, should I not return, he would take the ship with my blessing and start a new freelance career on his own.

225

Helinea's advertised diplomatic immunity was enough to ensure her ship landed on Fertilla without attracting the attention of the Fertillan Guard and it entered the spaceport at Londos without being searched. We joined the crew in boarding a personnel transport and we arrived at the Halls of the Deity without anyone searching the vehicle. The rest of the crew disembarked, but we stayed behind because we knew the Manupian security uniforms we wore would not be enough to stop us being recognised.

Stephen asked Helinea for one last favour, to send a member of the Fertillan Guard who he could trust out to the transport under the proviso of running a security sweep.

We sat facing each other in the dark on two rows of seats which ran down each side of the back of the vehicle. Neither of us spoke as we listened for the sound of the handle on the rear door being turned.

When the sound came, both of us leant back into the shadows as the door opened and daylight streamed inside from the compound behind the Halls of the Deity.

Standing silhouetted against the light was the figure of a woman in Fertillan Guard uniform. When she saw us, she pulled her EEW sidearm and aimed it in our direction.

"What are you doing in here?" she demanded, and I recognised a voice that I hadn't heard for a long time. "You are all supposed to have disembarked on arrival."

Stephen raised his hands and stepped forward so his face came out of the shadows and she could see him clearly. "It's good to see you, Louissi."

She gasped. "Commander Regellan?" Her voice was uncertain, but her aim was solid and her finger was ready on the trigger.

"What are you doing here? My orders are to arrest you on sight."

"I know, Louissi, but I asked you to come because I hoped you would be someone I could rely on to not act on those orders. At least, not immediately."

"Who's that with you?" She swung her EEW towards me.

I raised my hands and also stepped away from the side of the vehicle so she could see me.

"Cassy?" She peered closer, but her gun didn't waver. "I thought you had escaped."

"We wouldn't have come back here if it wasn't important, Louissi. Please come inside before someone sees you."

She looked around again. "Drakh!" She sighed. "I must be out of my mind."

She climbed inside. Stephen offered her a hand to help. She hesitated, but took it and kept her weapon well away from him in her other hand. Once she was inside, Stephen closed the doors and I felt a little bit safer.

I turned on the internal lights of the transport so they were at a low level and I was able to see Louissi's face between the stiff collar of her brown Fertillan Guard jacket and the peak of her cap pulled down low over her eyes. She seemed very skittish, and I didn't blame her. It had been a long time since she had let me go rather than hand me over to Prince James in the Jonsonii factory back on Manupia. Stephen had earmarked her out for promotion after that and he hoped that it was enough to ensure her loyalty. But it was still a gamble.

Stephen and I sat back down while Louissi remained standing. She still held her EEW, but she allowed her arm to rest down by her side so she was no longer pointing it at us.

"You do realise you are the two most wanted people on the planet and you are sitting outside a building with virtually every member of the Fertillan Guard either inside it or surrounding it?"

"Yes," said Stephen. "Which is why we need your help."

"No!" she said. "I can't help you! Prince James knew you favoured me before you were disgraced and he's made sure I've been sidelined at every opportunity. Even if I wanted to, I don't have the authority to do anything that could possibly help you."

"All we need," said Stephen, "are two sets of monk's robes and whatever details you can give us about security checkpoints inside the Halls."

"What? So you can shoot another member of the royal family? I won't be party to this. My life has been dragged through the drakh enough already."

"Louissi, please," I said. "I didn't shoot Queen Triana. It's why I'm here, to prove my innocence. But we need to get to the broadcast centre inside the Halls. It's where all the feeds from all the cameras are sent to be mixed before they're transmitted across the planet. Do you know where it is?"

"It's where it always is, in a suite on the floor above the viewing boxes in the main hall. But if you go in there disguised as monks, you can't take any weapons with you. The only people with EEWs are Fertillan Guards and they have all been vetted personally by Prince James."

"If I could go in there disguised as a member of the Fertillan Guard, I would," said Stephen. "Unfortunately, people are used to seeing me in the uniform."

"If you're discovered, you're more likely to be shot and killed than captured and arrested," said Louissi. "The whole of the Fertillan

Guard are twitchy after what happened last time."

"Let us worry about that," said Stephen. "The hood of a monk's robe should be enough to hide my face from a casual glance, and I also have these." He pulled a handkerchief from his pocket, unwrapped it and revealed the two small discs of the same brown contact lenses he had worn for our journey into cryo-sleep.

"So," I said. "Will you help us?"

"I can tell you about the security checkpoints and I can probably find two sets of monk's robes, but I'm not going to help you get inside. If you're caught, I will deny everything."

"That's all we ask," said Stephen.

Louissi turned to me. "You really weren't the assassin?"

"No," I said.

"I knew it as soon as you were arrested. Cassy couldn't have done it, I thought, she's much cleverer than that."

She turned to go, but Stephen called her back. "Louissi, can I just ask, who was put in charge of the Fertillan Guard after I left?"

"Bodlaine," she said.

"Bodlaine?" questioned Stephen. "Not Fedril or Preslondo? Surely they would have been better qualified."

"But they were loyal to you, Sire," said Louissi, using his honorific title out of habit. "Bodlaine's loyalty has always been to James. It was no surprise to those of us lower down the pecking order that he was given the top job. Everyone hates him. We call him Scarface behind his back."

"A strange nickname," said Stephen.

"Not really," said Louissi. "One of the guests at your wedding scratched him in the panic after the shooting. It left a nasty scar down his right cheek."

She left the transport and closed the doors behind her, but I barely noticed her leave. I was remembering the fight I had with the man in a monk's robes and how I had tried everything to get the rifle away from him.

"Stephen?" I said. "This man Bodlaine… did he not have a scar when you knew him?"

"Not that I remember. He was, as Louissi said, more loyal to James than me and I had little to do with him if I could help it. Does it matter?"

"It might matter," I said. "It might matter a great deal. Because, when I was fighting with the monk up in the box, I scratched his face. My nail went right into his cheek and, by the way he screamed, it makes me think it went deep enough to create a scar."

CHAPTER TWENTY NINE

THE MONK'S HOOD hid my face. The wraps that I had wound tightly around my breasts did much to hide my femininity while the robe completed the job by disguising the shape of my body.

I chose my moment to pass through the security checkpoint when the guards were distracted so they wouldn't look closely at my face, but I needn't have worried. They had confidence in their scanning equipment that showed that I was not armed and the belief that everyone who had entered the Halls of the Deity, including the monks, had been cleared by security checks at the entrances. They did not suspect that one of their most honoured guests, namely Helinea, would have used their superior security clearance to allow me and Stephen to bypass the very checks that were supposed to detect us.

We made our way to the broadcast suite where I stayed just long enough to make sure we had what we needed, then I left

Stephen and descended the two flights of stairs to the ground floor where the curved shape of a plain corridor followed the contour of the building. As I walked, I passed the same row of indistinguishable doors that I remembered from when the Fertillan guardsman had brought me to see Stephen on his wedding day that had ended so tragically.

No one stopped me. No one questioned me. I even passed a genuine monk going in the other direction, but he was in such a hurry to reach wherever he was going, that he didn't seem to notice that I didn't look up from under the fabric of the hood that shielded my identity.

I headed for the side door which I knew led to the main hall and slipped through to the other side where the dignitaries were taking part in their final rehearsal before James and Sophea were due to get married.

The main hall's grandeur was as spectacular as I remembered it. The underside of the domed roof which had been blasted by the assassin as I fought for control of his EE rifle had been restored and the globe light that hung from the centre once again sent out tiny rainbows from the cut glass encrusted into its surface. Drapes decorated the walls and rows upon rows of chairs lay either side of the aisle which led up to an empty stage. I smiled as I saw that, at strategic points of the hall, there were technicians with cameras rehearsing to make sure they captured everything when the big moment came.

Two men in Fertillan Guard uniform stood between me and the front of the hall where the essential members of the wedding parties had gathered. Between the outlines of their bodies, I could see the backs of a man and a woman who appeared to be James and Sophea standing next to each other like Stephen and Helinea had done when they walked up the aisle. In front of them was the same Supreme Monk who had presided over the first ceremony, dressed in the same white robe. Helinea was standing off to one side surrounded by several Manupian security officials while a man in Fertillan Guard uniform stood off to the other side. By the cut of his uniform, which was smoother and more tailored than the standard clothes given to the enlisted guards, I suspected it was Bodlaine.

I couldn't see King Richard, but I could hear that he was standing somewhere between James and Sophea and the stage. It was impossible not to hear him. He sounded so angry that his voice boomed across the hall.

"I am *not* standing on the stage," he was insisting. "We are going to have the *choir* on the stage."

"But it's important for everyone to see that you endorse this marriage." It was Prince James's voice. I couldn't see his face, because he had his back to me, but it sounded like he was struggling to keep his irritation with his brother under control. "That is why we have the stage."

"This is why we have the *cameras*," said King Richard. "I can sit in the front row and be seen on camera as much as if I were on the stage. I don't care what kind of argument you put forward, James, I am *not* standing in the same spot where my wife was killed so soon after I watched her body – and that of my son – cremated into ashes."

I reached the two guards who blocked my path and was forced to stop.

"I need to see the King," I said. My voice gave me away as being female, but it didn't matter any more. I was where I needed to be.

The guard to my left, evidently somewhat distracted by the royal arguments going on behind him, leant forward and said to me quietly: "No monks beyond this point. This is a private rehearsal."

"But I need to see the King!" I raised my voice so they all could hear. "I know who assassinated the Queen and I can prove it!"

"Who is this annoying monk?" demanded King Richard. "Get him away from here!"

James turned and, as I skipped backwards to avoid being man-handled by the guards attempting to usher me out, he saw directly into my eyes. "It's Sesaan Cassandra!" he shouted. "The assassin!"

But I was ready for him. I was not there for him to unmask me. I was there to unmask myself.

I grabbed hold of my hood and pulled it back off my head to reveal my face. "I have come to protest my innocence and pledge my allegiance to you, Your Majesty. You must know that I would never–"

James pushed the two guards aside and lunged towards me. I turned to escape, but his hand grabbed my robe and jerked me back. My feet scrabbled for a foothold on the floor, slipping on its smooth surface, and I fell backwards with James still holding on tight to the fabric of my robe. He pushed me to the ground, turned me over roughly and pressed my face so hard into the floor that I smelled the polish that had been used to make it slippery. I felt other hands grab my arms and force them behind my back. Soon, I felt the familiar cold encasement of metal handcuffs securing my wrists.

It was what I had expected. My job was to walk into the hall and get everyone's attention. As James pulled me to my knees and I looked into the other faces from the two ruling households

– Richard, Sophea, Helinea – and their assembled security personnel, I knew I had achieved my aim.

"Your Majesty," I said to the King, who was walking down the aisle towards me. "I tried to stop the man who killed Queen Triana. I swear on my life. I would not have come back if–"

He lifted his hand and I turned my face as I thought he was about to strike me. But, instead, he grabbed my hair – pulling it painfully from the roots – and yanked my head back to expose my throat.

"Give me your weapon!" he demanded of one of the guardsmen.

"Your Majesty?" the man stuttered.

"Your EEW! *Now!*"

Richard thrust out his hand, the guard fumbled to pass over his sidearm and I felt the pressure of the end of its small barrel against the side of my skull. The dread of impending death pushed my heart to beat at its maximum, I gasped panicked breaths as I feared my plan was about to go disastrously wrong.

I had thought they might detain me, I thought they might beat me, I thought they might arrest me, but I didn't think they would shoot me. Not in front of the distinguished guests of the wedding party. But in all my calculations, I hadn't allowed for the strength of King Richard's grief.

"You killed my wife and my child." He spat into my face and saliva ran down my cheek.

"I swear, I did not."

"Do you know how many sleepless nights I have fantacised about being in this position with you at my mercy?"

I swallowed. Fear had stolen my words. The gun pressed harder into my head and I prepared myself for the inevitable.

"Let us hear what she has to say first," said the voice of my saviour: Helinea. She walked down the aisle, with her shoes tapping gently on the floor until I could see her standing in front of me.

"But she is the assassin," said Richard.

"She says she isn't," said Helinea. "Which means she's either very suicidal or what she has to say might be worth listening to."

Richard threw my head forward and let go of my hair. The barrel of the EEW was no longer pressed against my skull and I gasped more precious moments of my life.

"Speak," he ordered.

I cleared my throat and recited my prepared speech through my anxious, dry mouth. "I only went into the box because I was looking for somewhere to watch the ceremony." I looked up beside me to the very box where I had struggled with the monk. "I didn't know until the man arrived that someone had planned to use it for a different purpose – it was the ideal vantage point for an assassin. I didn't realise what he was going to do until I saw the rifle under his monk's robes. I fought to get it off him, but I am very sorry, Your Majesty, I was unable to stop him before he killed your wife."

"We've heard this story before!" scoffed James from behind me. "It has all been discredited."

But, as he spoke, the P-tabs belonging to everyone in the hall spontaneously came to life. Their screens lit up and their little speakers played the sound of a hall full of people singing the Fertillan anthem. I watched their confused faces as they reached into their pockets and pulled out their devices.

"I said, I have proof," I told them. "Everything was recorded by one of the cameras in the hall. If people hadn't been so keen to convict me, they might have looked at the evidence."

Everyone was looking now. They all had their P-tabs in their hands and were watching the screens. As I heard the verse of the anthem approach the rousing chorus from more than a dozen little speakers around me, I knew they were watching the images from the one camera that had been pointing in my direction. The camera that had seen how the man in monk's clothing rested the barrel of his rifle on the edge of the balcony. It had seen the blur of my blue dress as I barged into him to try to stop him and it had recorded the bright streak of energy fire out of the box heading in the direction of an innocent woman and her unborn baby.

"Who's doing this?" demanded James. "How are they doing this?"

But no one was listening. They were all watching.

Then, through the speakers, came Stephen's voice over the top of the original audio. "In this footage recorded by one of the official cameras placed to capture the events of the wedding, we can see that Sesaan Cassandra was not the assassin. If we zoom in, we can see that it was – as she claimed – a man dressed as a monk. Unfortunately, the footage only shows his face in shadow or hidden by the hood of his monk's robe…"

The Fertillan Guard who I suspected was Bodlaine stepped into the aisle. "Sire!" he called out towards James. "The voice, Sire, it's Prince Stephen." He pushed past the others who were standing in his way, apologising as he went until he stood in front of me. I could clearly see the scar that I had scratched into his cheek.

"Of course it's Stephen!" barked James, tugging at the neck of my robe and forcing me back like I was some kind of animal on his leash.

"His security clearance to transmit on an emergency channel to all P-tabs must still be active, Sire," said Bodlaine.

"But transmit from where?" said James.

"He has to be in the broadcast centre in the Halls, Sire. It explains where he obtained the footage."

James pushed me forward dismissively and I felt his stranglehold on my robe release. "Keep an eye on her, Bodlaine. I'll deal with Stephen."

Still on my knees, I heard James run back down the aisle and throw open the side door that led to the two flights of steps which would take him to the broadcast centre.

The footage being broadcast to everyone's P-tab in the vicinity continued to play in a loop and, one by one, people stopped watching it. Helinea and Sophea had already left with their contingent of Manupian security officials, along with the Supreme Monk. The technicians who had been there to rehearse their camera moves had also fled, leaving their equipment behind. Only the Fertillans had stayed.

Bodlaine kept his hand firmly on my shoulder as I knelt, uncomfortably, on my knees. The two guards who had blocked my path, stood on either side of the aisle as if uncertain of what their role should be. King Richard, meanwhile, was sitting on one of the empty chairs with his head bowed in front of him. I couldn't imagine what was going through his mind. The story he had been told when I was arrested, of who had killed his wife and why, had just been torn to shreds in front of him.

The side door opened and Stephen was shoved through it. Blood dripped from his nose down to his mouth and, although he still wore monk's robes, they had been torn down the front and the white of his shirt was showing through. James had twisted Stephen's arm up behind his back so hard that I could see the pain on his face as he was forced to walk in front of his brother.

When they reached me, James thrust him forward and Stephen fell onto his knees. One of his brown contact lenses had fallen out and, when he recovered himself and looked across at me, it was with different coloured eyes.

"Are you okay, Cassy?" he asked.

"For now," I said.

It was only then that King Richard raised his head. He looked in our direction and the glassiness of his eyes revealed a heartache greater than tears could express.

"Is it true, Stephen?" he said, holding up the P-tab he had been watching.

"It's true, Richard," said Stephen.

"But why? Was it Manupian terrorists? Did he mean to shoot President Sophea and hit my Triana by mistake?"

"I don't believe so," said Stephen. "I think he meant to kill Triana all along."

"Liar!" came James's outburst from behind us. "Even on his knees before the King he lies." James kicked Stephen in the back and he doubled up in pain.

"James!" said Richard, standing to assert his authority. "Control yourself. This is where my wife died. Have some respect."

"You asked if it was Manupian terrorists," I said. "But that was just a clever decoy. The truth is, I know who the assassin is because, when I was wrestling to gain control of the rifle, I scratched his cheek."

Richard's gaze switched from looking at James to looking at Bodlaine.

Bodlaine's hand left my shoulder and, as I looked up at him, I saw him place his palm over his scar.

"Your Majesty," he said. "The woman is merely making up a story to throw suspicion off herself. Everyone knows that I was scratched in the panic when everyone fled the Halls after the shooting."

"If it wasn't you, then run a DNA test on the samples taken from me when I was arrested," I said. "I scraped off plenty of your skin under my fingernail. Or they could test the rifle you planted on me. Perhaps you wiped it clean of all traces of yourself before you fled the scene or perhaps you didn't."

Richard was staring at Bodlaine. By the expression on his face, I knew that he needed no DNA test to prove that what I said was true. "*Why?* For the Deity's sake, *why?*"

Bodlaine smiled. It was such a perverse reaction after such a horrific accusation that it was like he didn't understand what I was saying. Like he was still trying to make sense of how the walls of his defence could have crumbled so quickly. "I didn't want to do it, Your Majesty, you must believe me. But I am loyal to Fertilla and I was following orders."

"Someone ordered you?" said Richard with remarkable calmness. "Who? Who ordered you?"

"James, Your Majesty," Bodlaine stuttered. "It was Prince James."

Richard said nothing. He merely stared at his twin brother with hard, narrowed eyes.

"You don't believe him?" said James with incredulity. "He's clearly trying to save himself."

At that moment, the main doors to the hall opened and a squadron of Fertillan Guard marched in. There were at least ten of them.

"Excuse the interruption, Your Majesty," said a tall woman who seemed to be leading them. "But President Sophea said you might be needing some assistance."

"Arrest these two!" said Richard, pointing at James and Bodlaine.

The woman hesitated. "Prince James and Marshal Commander Bodlaine?"

"Arrest them and lock them in the deepest, darkest cell you can find."

Bodlaine made a bolt for it and dashed past Richard. He jumped onto the stage and disappeared behind a side curtain where there was probably some sort of stage door. Five of the guards who had just arrived chased after him, while the tall woman barked orders into her communicator that Bodlaine was to be stopped on sight.

The two guards who had been watching the whole thing unfold from the beginning, stepped alongside James. The tall woman led the rest of her squadron towards him from the rear. "Put your hands behind you back, Sire," she said.

James ignored her and made his appeals to the King. "But, Richard, I am your *brother*."

The woman grabbed his hands and pulled them behind him where they were secured with a set of handcuffs. James didn't resist. He didn't even seem to be aware of what was happening.

"I know you coveted the throne, James, but assassinating a pregnant woman… How can my own brother have sunk so low?"

said Richard. "What did you have planned for me? Poison in my tea or were you planning to push me down the stairs and claim it was an accident?"

James showed no emotion as he was led away by the guards. Only two of them remained and stood to attention as if on sentry duty.

Richard held out his hand to Stephen. Stephen took it and allowed his brother to help him to his feet. "You risked a great deal today," he said.

"I wanted to see justice done," said Stephen. He bent down, took my arm and helped me to my feet. Even though my hands were still secured behind me, I felt more free than I could remember in a long time.

"What can I do for you in return?" said Richard.

"A royal pardon for me and Cassy."

Richard looked at Stephen and then to me. He nodded. "I'm sure that can be arranged," he said.

CHAPTER THIRTY

I STOOD IN THE control room of the Fertillan Guard ship, Regellan One, with Stephen at my side. He was in command, but had dispensed with his Fertillan Guard uniform as he said he didn't feel comfortable in it any more. Helinea was with us as we watched the giant screen that dominated the room and showed the view out of the front of the ship. There were no stars, only blackness, because we had reached the edge of the galaxy and were staring into the barrier.

The uniformed members of Stephen's crew busied themselves at their consoles. There were so many of them compared to my small crew that consisted of only me and Freddi, that I wondered how they could all keep occupied. Nevertheless, they didn't seem to have time to pay much attention to Helinea and myself as they watched the fluctuating data on their consoles which I knew from experience was nothing like they would have ever seen before.

A curl of green light flashed out of the barrier on the screen for just an instant before it was gone. Blackness remained for only another second before there was a flash of blue and then red light. The flashes became more frequent and more elaborate until there were multiple colours all swirling and twisting in a majestic light show in front of us.

"Is this it?" said Helinea.

"This is it," I told her.

The crew began to call out the readings they were seeing. Some of them with concern, some of them with bewilderment, but Stephen simply let the noise play out around him. He, like us, knew what the light show meant and it was something to be celebrated, not feared.

The first of the hemispheres of Eden began to break through. The edge of the dome sliced through the barrier like a scythe through wheat and its bulbous shape followed until all of it was inside the Obsidian Rim. Behind it, came the rest of the ship. The central core and the four other domes emerged with a halo of the barrier's lights sparking around it like a firework display. As it came closer to us, the lights faded and the ship emerged undamaged into our galaxy after many generations in exile.

Stephen's crew burst into applause. They had never seen something pass through the barrier before and they had witnessed something that they had been taught, from childhood, was impossible. I lifted my hands to clap along with them and I saw Helinea do the same. Stephen just stood grinning with his hands clasped behind his back.

"Let's get communications on the main speakers," Stephen ordered one of his subordinates and the applause died down.

"Yes, Commander," came the reply and hush descended on the control room as the hiss of static was conveyed all around us.

Stephen approached the nearest console. A small woman in uniform stepped dutifully aside for him. He leant over and activated the communication control. "This is Regellan One to Eden. Can you hear me?"

Hiss responded. Tension rose among the enlisted personnel.

Stephen, steadily and calmly, repeated his hail. "This is Regellan One to Eden. Please respond."

In the jumble of interference, several syllables broke through. "…den… ling… Reg… One."

I exchanged glances with Helinea. The crew stared straight ahead with expectant faces.

"Repeat your message, Eden," said Stephen.

"…is Eden calling Regellan One," said Freddi's voice loud and clear. I breathed deep with relief, although I never doubted for a second that he could bring the vessel safely through. "It's good to hear your voice, Stephen."

Some of the crew smirked.

"So informal, Freddi?" said Stephen into the communicator.

"I meant, good to hear your voice, Marshal Commander Regellan. I'll move a little closer to you and then I'll return in your shuttle."

"Looking forward to seeing you."

"I'll be bringing Doctor Keya Sharma," said Freddi. "She has requested to go back to Fertilla with you to start work bringing together a scientific team to exploit the food technology on other worlds."

"Terri and Malcon are happy to stay there?"

"They said they need to be around when other people arrive to examine Eden. I don't think they want to leave any time soon."

"Understood," said Stephen.

"Then I look forward to seeing her too."

Helinea stepped forward and whispered something in his ear. Stephen nodded. "Helinea also reminds you that you promised to bring over some of the food from Eden. Apparently, she's heard good things about your cooking and wants to see if they are true."

"Tell Cassy, she has a big mouth," said Freddi.

I smiled.

A steady, but persistent bleeping could be heard in the background of Freddi's transmission. "I need to go. I'll be in touch again when we've reached position. Eden out."

The communication went dead.

Helinea looked uncertainly between Stephen and me. "Is everything all right?"

"A ship like that takes a lot of flying," said Stephen. "It's best we leave him to concentrate."

"Freddi is an experienced pilot," I told her. "Getting through the barrier was the hard part. The rest is relatively straight forward."

It was why we had come in the first place.

The future of Eden was now in the joint hands of the Fertillans and the Manupians. Regellan One, and its crew, were perfectly capable of travelling through the galaxy and boarding Eden, but only Freddi had ever taken a ship through the barrier. He had agreed to lend them his expertise for that final task, which was why we had followed Stephen in our own ship and I had come aboard while Freddi had taken their shuttle.

Our plan always was to leave soon after. We had no appetite for hanging around while Stephen's engineers carried out their examinations and various experts had discussions about what to do with Eden's plant life. I had bills to pay and, after so long without taking on a freelance job, I needed to get back in the game as soon as possible.

So, we would enjoy one last meal with Stephen and Helinea – and also, it turned out, Keya – and then we would say goodbye.

Although, how I was going to say goodbye to Stephen, after we had grown so close in recent weeks, was still something I was yet to work out.

STEPHEN'S QUARTERS WERE sparse and practical and befitting the military man they were supposed to serve. There was a desk with a screen, an upright chair suitable for working rather than relaxing in, a narrow wardrobe with four sets of the tailored Fertillan Guard uniform he said he no longer felt comfortable wearing and only one change of civilian clothes. A small washroom was attached with all the basics and nothing more, but it was the single bed that spoke most about his life aboard ship. It was only as big as it needed to be for a man to sleep in and do nothing else.

I was sitting at his desk, going through some of the data which Freddi had brought across from Eden, when Stephen came in.

He closed the door behind him and leant back on it with a heavy sigh. He looked tired. He had taken off his jacket and undone the top button of his shirt.

"Sorry I was so long, Cassy."

I turned off the screen and got up from the desk. "I'm sure it was important."

"It's not good news on Eden's QED. Freddi's been talking to my chief engineer and the long and short of it is that it will take a team of experts to take a serious look at the drive before they can even think of activating it."

"Well, that's okay. That's what you brought them for, isn't it?"

"Yes, but it means the ship needs to stick around out here longer than I'd planned. I could leave the team on Eden and travel back to Fertilla without them, but I'd rather not. We have facilities and equipment here that… well, shall we say it will be more practical for them if we stay. We need to know if Eden is capable of wormhole travel or whether we'll have to find some way of transporting everything in other ships. Keya doesn't want to cause too much disruption to the hemispheres, but if Eden is only capable of normal space travel, then we might have no choice."

I approached him, cupped his chin in my hand, felt the roughness of the stubble that had grown there after a long day and brought him close so I could kiss him.

His lips softened and I tasted the sensuousness of his body. We kissed for many minutes until, reluctantly, he pulled away.

"I have to ask you for a favour, Cassy."

"Of course."

"When you and Freddi leave in your ship, can you take me, Helinea and Keya back to Fertilla?"

"You're always welcome on my ship, Stephen, you know that. But Freddi and I thought we'd go to Rega to find work. There's supposed to be some easy freight jobs going that pay decent rates."

"I'll pay for you to take us," said Stephen. "Consider it your last freelance job for me."

"A lucrative passenger run? I'm sure we can manage that." I stepped away from him and began unbuttoning my shirt to reveal my neck, then my collarbone, then the top of my cleavage. "You know the other thing that coming back to my ship will mean?"

"No, what's that?"

"Having access to a decent-sized bed."

I laughed and he came towards me, unable to resist my strip-tease any further. He undid two more buttons so my breasts were displayed before him. I reached for his shirt, desperate to release his nakedness and feel it next to mine. But it was quicker and easier to undress ourselves and so we pulled off our own clothes and fell onto the small platform of Stephen's bed. Its strong, military mattress barely softened under our weight, but we had each other and that was the only comfort we needed.

His strong arms held me to stop me falling off the edge and we kissed again. My lips tingled as my breasts were pressed against his chest and my nipples stood to attention at his command. I allowed my hand to drift down his side to find the tight curve of his buttock and squeezed to encourage our bodies to become closer.

Our lovemaking was slower than the desperate passion we had let loose after drinking Malcon's wine back on Eden, but we succumbed to it just as deeply. We took our time to enjoy each other, to feel the desire building and the excitement rising until we were alive with sex. Only then did we allow our bodies to come together and climax in an explosion that rippled through to every nerve ending. Like I was the edge of the galaxy and he was the ship which broke through with an eruption of fireworks.

My sighs of satisfaction were not as loud as my screams on Eden, but they went deeper and said more than a simple orgasm ever could. It was not only the ecstasy of sex that I was sharing with a man, it was the total honesty of my naked body that I was able to share with Stephen without reservation.

I lay back on the bed afterwards, forgetting how narrow it was and nearly toppled over the side. I laughed as Stephen grabbed me and pulled me tightly to him.

"I don't think they had couples in mind when they designed your quarters," I said, as I felt myself coming down and my heightened senses begin to be aware of the room again.

"I think the idea was that I should keep my mind on running the ship."

"Life in the Fertillan Guard sounds so boring."

"It can be," he said with all seriousness.

We lay there for a little longer until the relative chill of the room sent us scuttling under the covers. I rested my head on his chest and felt the steady thump of his heartbeat beneath my cheek.

"A year ago, I told myself I would never sleep with you again," I said, thinking back to the time that I had forced myself to forget about him.

"I'm sorry that didn't work out for you," he said.

"So, what do I do now? Keep coming back to your bedchamber in Londos House every time we're in the system? That's not going to satisfy me, it's not going to satisfy you and I know Freddi will hate it."

"I'm sorry I pulled you back into this relationship, Cassy. It wasn't part of any grand plan."

"Don't be sorry. You broke me out of jail. If it hadn't been for you, I would still be locked in that cell. Convicted of treason and executed by now, probably."

"But if I hadn't invited you to my wedding, you wouldn't have been there in the first place."

"Then the assassin would have got away with it and James would be poised to seize power." I sighed. "We could go on like this, until we went back to the creation of the universe. It's not really anyone's fault, it's just what happened."

"Yes," said Stephen, in thought. "I suppose you're asking me what we should do now."

"I suppose I am," I said.

"I don't know, Cassy." He brushed my hair away from my forehead and kissed my smooth skin. "But we'll find a way."

CHAPTER THIRTY ONE

FREDDI'S COOKING WAS, as always, amazing.

We had elected to return to my ship to eat, rather than stay on Stephen's ship, because it gave us the chance to make an early start back to Fertilla. It allowed Freddi to cook in facilities which were more familiar to him while our engines moved us through normal space to a point where we could safely engage our QED, away from both Regellan One and the barrier. It also meant he was under no pressure to cater for the rest of Stephen's crew.

Keya and Helinea seemed to have a rapport the moment they met. It was like they were childhood friends suddenly reunited and had two lifetimes' worth of experiences to catch up on. They talked and they talked and they talked. Other than the occasional, "can you pass the flatbreads?" during the meal, they barely said a word to the rest of us.

It was while we were eating that Ellen, the ship's computer, informed us that we had reached an appropriate position where

QED travel could be initiated and she had brought us to a full stop. Freddi slipped away from the festivities at that point to start work on the calculations to take us back to Fertilla. A little while after, while Stephen was distracted helping himself to the last of one of Freddi's stews, I slipped out to join him.

The control room was quiet when I got there. There was just Freddi, with his head down over his console, working on his calculations. It seemed normal. Like all the events since we had left to go to Stephen's wedding had never happened.

Freddi glanced up from his work. "Has the meal finished?" he asked me.

"Almost," I said. "Keya and Helinea are still talking. I think they have everything they plan to do over the next twenty years worked out already."

He smiled and went back to his calculations.

I walked over to my console and brought up the details of our trip through the wormhole. It was a simple, straight forward journey and similar to ones we had taken many times before.

"When I left Fertilla to make a life for myself out in space, I didn't imagine I would be going back there so often," I said.

"Me neither," said Freddi. "This time it's actually useful for me because, before I left, I got word that Ange is getting married. This trip means I'll be able to be there for the ceremony."

His announcement took me totally by surprise. "Your daughter? Congratulations."

"Thanks. She met some hunky farmer at some agricultural conference or something. I wasn't able to get all of the details, but I gather she's going to be moving onto his farm."

"What about your other daughter?"

"Jan? She'll still be running my old farm. I have no doubt she can manage on her own and, with Ange gone, it will allow her to think more about her own future. I have no idea if she'll get married or even if she wants to."

"That's good then," I said. "This passenger run is working out for everyone. Stephen's payment is going to be really useful."

"What are you going to do about Stephen? You know, if we take on other jobs, you won't have many opportunities to visit him."

I rolled my eyes. It was the question I had been asking myself and one to which I didn't have an answer. "I don't know. He's back being a prince and I'm going to go back to being a freelance space-ship captain. It's like trying to mix oil and water."

I started as I heard Stephen enter the control room. He appeared content and comfortable. He had his hands casually resting inside the pockets of his trousers and the sleeves of his jacket pushed up to almost his elbow. The top button of his shirt was undone to reveal a single hair which I knew was one of many that adorned his chest. He looked so much more attractive in civilian clothes than he had ever done in his Fertillan Guard uniform. But it was his blue eyes, as he looked at me, which were the most handsome thing about him. I felt a little bit of excitement as his gaze warmed my insides like no other man could.

"What's oil and water?" he said.

I wasn't sure how much of our conversation he had overheard, but I decided to deflect his question with one of my own. "Has everyone finished the meal?"

"I left Keya and Helinea talking," he said. "They were getting into specific details about preserving seed and it was starting not to make any sense to me."

I smiled. I had felt the same when I had listened to part of their conversation before I left to find Freddi.

"Are we about ready to wormhole back to Fertilla?" Stephen asked.

"Almost," said Freddi. "In fact, Cassy, you should probably tell the others to prepare."

I accessed the communications control on my screen and turned on all the speakers throughout the ship. "Keya and Helinea, this is Cassy. We're getting ready to engage the QED and travel through the wormhole back to Fertilla. You should find somewhere to make yourself comfortable. If you could secure all the bowls, plates and cutlery in the crew lounge first, that would be a big help."

Freddi looked up from his console. Evidently, he had finished his calculations and everything was set.

"So, Stephen," he said. "What are you planning to do when you get home?"

"Home," said Stephen, taking a moment to consider the thought. "For a long time, I thought I wouldn't be able to call Londos House my home again. I'm sure it's going to be busy when I get there. There's James's trial, of course. I am required to be a witness at that. I also need to set in place arrangements to work closely with Manupia on the food project. But I was thinking Fedril or Preslondo can handle that. In fact, I was thinking of promoting one of them to the head of the Fertillan Guard and stepping down completely."

"But Stephen," I said. "That's your job."

"Yes it is, but I don't think I want it to be any longer. These last few weeks with you, Cassy... Well, it would be wrong to say they have been entirely enjoyable. I've been handcuffed by my own personnel, nearly been killed at least twice and damn near had my nose broken by my own brother, but being back in charge of Regellan One on the journey out to retrieve Eden didn't seem right. I was uncomfortable with everyone saying 'yes, Sire' all the time. In fact, I was thinking… Cassy, if you don't mind… I would like to travel with you."

He looked directly at me with his beautiful, blue penetrating eyes and – for a moment – I stopped breathing. It was everything I wanted, but I always thought such a dream was impossible. "But your duty…"

"My duty no longer matters," said Stephen. "At least, not to me. Richard will understand. He loved a woman who he lost because she was violently taken away from him. After everything that has happened, he will agree to my request."

I started breathing again, but only because if I didn't, I would pass out. My whole body tingled with excitement. It was like sex, but somehow fulfilling in a more meaningful way.

I left the console, ran up to him and kissed him so passionately that it was difficult to let him go.

When I emerged from our embrace, I turned to see Freddi watching us.

"Oh Freddi," I said. I knew that bringing Stephen on board permanently would be difficult. We were a team, Freddi and I, and adding a third person to the crew risked unbalancing our working relationship. Especially as the new crew member would be a man used to commanding a ship full of personnel. "I should ask you what you think. I want to say yes, but…"

"Then you should say yes, Cassy," he said.

"You would be okay with it? Really?"

"Actually, Cassy…" Freddi bowed his head, like he was embarrassed. But when he lifted his eyes to look at me again, there was a seriousness in his expression. "When I collected you and Stephen from Patti's ship after you escaped from Fertilla, she asked me again to join her on her ship. I didn't say no this time. I said I would think about it. Well, I've thought about it and I've decided I'd like to accept her offer."

"Freddi, you're going to leave?" As I said it, I felt the tears coming. It was the perfect solution, but it was heartbreaking at the same time.

"I think it's time."

I left Stephen's side and ran up to Freddi. I hugged him and felt him stiffen uncomfortably against my embrace, but I held him tight anyway. He put his arms around me for a moment, then pulled me back.

When he did so, I felt the coolness of air on the tears that had run down my cheeks and was well aware that he could see them.

"Hey, Cassy," he said. "I'm leaving, not dying."

He wiped the moisture away from my face with his shirt sleeve and, he was so gentle, it made more tears come.

"I know," I said, sniffing to clear my airway. "But you've always been here. We've always travelled together. I can't imagine working on a spaceship without you."

"You'll cope," he said.

I nodded.

"Even if Stephen's not as good a pilot as me."

"No."

"Or as good an engineer."

"No."

"His cooking is probably lousy as well."

I laughed through my tears. "Probably."

"In fact, it's going to be really tough without me."

He was joking, but in some ways – many ways – he was right. "Yes."

"But this is best," he said. "For all of us."

Ellen's voice broke in from the speakers above. "We are ready to engage the Quantum Entanglement Drive. Any further delay could cause the preparatory calculations to be inaccurate."

Freddi's eyes lifted to the ceiling where the speakers were embedded. "Thank you, Ellen."

I went back to Stephen's side while Freddi made the final arrangements and set our path in motion.

"Q-burst initiating," said Ellen.

I held onto Stephen as a rumble like approaching thunder engulfed the ship. He put his hands gently on my waist and leant forward to kiss me. As our lips touched, the QED engaged and the joy of us being together eclipsed the usual pain of wormhole travel, as a rift was created through spacetime and the ship was hurled across light years to reach our destination.

* * *

COMING IN 2020...

THE ECHOES SERIES

Kirsty sees echoes of the future she can't change
– until she saves a man from certain death and
realises the future lies in her hands.

A new series of books from Jane Killick

ALSO BY JANE KILLICK

PERCEIVERS

Mind Secrets

Mind Control

Mind Evolution

Mind Power

Teenagers with special powers fight to exist
in a world that doesn't want them.

The complete series